It Wasn't All Dancing

and other stories

A Deep South Book

It Wasn't All Dancing

and other stories

MARY WARD BROWN

For "Dr. Bubba" Draughon
With love,

Mary Ward Brown

7/28/11

THE UNIVERSITY OF ALABAMA PRESS • TUSCALOOSA AND LONDON

9 8 7 6 5 4 3 2 1
10 09 08 07 06 05 04 03 02

Designer: Michele Myatt Quinn
Typeface: Garamond

Some of these stories originally appeared in the following
publications: "Alone in a Foreign Country" in *Five Points*
(Georgia State University); "A Meeting on the Road" in *The
Threepenny Review;* "No Sound in the Night" in *The Caroli-
na Quarterly;* "Once in a Lifetime" in *Many Voices, Many
Rooms* (University of Alabama Press); "The House That Asa
Built" in *University of Kansas City Review;* "A New Life" in
Atlantic Monthly; "It Wasn't All Dancing" in *Grand Street;*
and "The Birthday Cake" in *The Threepenny Review.*

Library of Congress Cataloging-in-Publication Data

Brown, Mary Ward.
    It wasn't all dancing and other stories / Mary Ward Brown.
        p.   cm. — (Deep South books)
    ISBN 0-8173-1124-6 (alk. paper)
    1. Southern States—Social life and customs—Fiction. I.
Title. II. Series.
    PS3552.R6944 I8 2002
    813'.54—dc21   2001003525

British Library Cataloguing-in-Publication Data available

To the memory of Charles Kirtley Brown

Contents

It Wasn't All Dancing

and other stories

✍ It Wasn't All Dancing

IN THE MORNING a strange black girl in white uniform stood by
Rose Merriweather's bed. Even her shoes and stockings were white.
Like a fly in a bucket of buttermilk, Rose's mother would have said
years ago. Rose's mother had been a St. Clair of Mobile, who had
married a Pardue from the Canebrake, a family just as good or better.

"I'm Rose Pardue, of Rosemont," Rose had introduced herself as
a girl. It had been her open sesame all over the Black Belt of Alabama. She fixed her once-famous eyes on the girl by her bed.

"Who are you, may I ask?"

"Your new nurse," the girl said pleasantly.

Rose pushed herself up on the pillow. The girl had a confident
smile, quick eyes, small hard-muscled body.

"What became of the other one?" Rose asked.

"Your daughter let her go." The girl picked up a Kleenex from
the rug, dropped it into the wastebasket Rose had missed.

Rose sighed. No sooner did she become used to one than
Catherine fired her or she quit.

"Help me to the bathroom, please," she said

This trip was the hardest of the day, since her muscles and joints had stiffened while she slept; but the girl was strong, steady, and kept her mouth shut. Once inside, Rose held on to the safety rail put up when she broke her hip.

"You can step out and shut the door now," she said.

The girl didn't move. "Your daughter said to don't never leave you."

"My daughter's not here, though, is she?" Rose raised one eyebrow and wiggled it, an old trick of hers. She was a beauty, people had said in her day, but also fun. In demand every minute. Her father, a tease, had called her the "Sigma Chi Sweetie," though her hair wasn't gold, her eyes not the blue of the song, and her beaus mostly SAEs and Phi Delta Thetas. Her eyes had been "dark and mysterious." Like sapphires, she'd been told.

The girl turned and went out, closing the door behind her. Straight face. No smile.

Back in bed, a cup of steaming coffee in her hand, Rose watched her new companion transfer a small Spode coffeepot from tray to bedside table. The pot was from a breakfast set Rose had forgotten she ever owned.

Nervy of the girl to get it out, though, she thought. And what if she broke it? Well, Catherine wouldn't want those dishes anyway, just because they'd been hers. Might as well use and enjoy them.

"What's your name, new nurse?" she asked.

"Etta. Etta Mae Jones." Slight pause. "You ready for some breakfast?"

Rose had already placed herself for the day. This was her own tester bed in her own house—hers and Allen's, though Allen had been dead for years now. Some days she thought she was back in the country, back in the home of her childhood, in spite of the fact that she knew very well that house was no longer even in the family. At other times, her problem was worse. She'd wake up to find several days had gone by without her knowing anything about it. There would be Monday and Tuesday, then nothing at all until Friday. Wednesday and Thursday would be wiped out completely.

The doctor wouldn't tell her what was wrong with her, if he knew, except that he thought it was age-related.

"How old did you say you were?" he would ask, a sudden twinkle in his eyes.

She would look at him, as over the edge of a fan. "I didn't say," she would tell him.

She'd get a new pill of a different color. "Don't worry, sweetheart. You're all right. You could outlive us all."

The tray Etta brought was set with more Spode, and good silver. There was orange juice in a pressed glass tumbler, a soft-boiled egg with toast and crisp bacon. Everything just right, as in the days of trained servants, and Rose was suddenly hungry. Starving.

"Very good!" she said, when Etta came back for the well-cleaned tray. "Thank you." She pointed to the egg cup. "I haven't seen one of these in years. I'm surprised you knew what it was."

Etta looked at her directly. "Mrs. Fitzhugh Greene, that I stayed with so long, wouldn't have her egg no other way," she said.

"But where'd you find all these dishes?"

"You don't know?" Tiny night lights seemed to come on in the dark of Etta's eyes. Her face lit up. "You got a jewe'ry store, right there in your kitchen. All kinds of stuff up in them cabinets. I been with rich folks before, but they didn't have what you got."

Rose had stopped breathing to listen, her mouth half-open. "It's old stuff too, some of it," she said. "Handed down in the family. It couldn't be replaced at any price, ever. Besides the sentimental value . . . Did my daughter tell you?"

Across a gulf of sudden silence, they looked at each other. Only their eyes seemed involved.

"You thinking about do I steal," Etta said, unexpectedly.

Rose's mouth went dry. She had no idea what to say.

"You don't have to worry, Mrs. Merriweather." Etta flashed out the words like a switchblade. "I don't take nothing. And on top of that, you don't have nothing I want."

She picked up the tray without rattling a dish, but her mouth was set, her eyes wide open. Holding the tray up protectively, she gave the door to the hall, which stood halfway open, a jab of the hip like a boxer's punch. Without looking back, she sailed out of sight.

Heavenly days! Rose thought. How did that come about? And what if she quit? Rose was ready to explain, apologize, beg if necessary. Anything not to lose her.

Down the hall, pots and pans began to rattle. Water ran through pipes. A dishwasher was turned on. When Etta came back, the expression she'd worn from the room had been erased. She picked up a nightgown as if nothing had happened.

So talent was touchy, Rose thought; and now black was touchy too, it seemed.

At last she got up the nerve to ask, "Etta, if there's nothing here that you want, what do you want in this world?"

"Nothing in nobody's house," said Etta, her interest obviously leftover and cold by now. Her attention was on all the pill bottles, empty glasses and neglected laundry scattered about.

"That girl left this place in a mess," she said.

Later in the day, as part of the routine, Rose sat up in a chair. Once settled, she turned her face toward the window. It was October and the leaves outside, though doomed, were still on the trees. Through blue autumn haze, the sky was like the tinted windshield of a car. She sat for a while without speaking, a far-centered look in her eyes.

"You think I'm rich, Etta?" she said at last, her voice like that of an old blues singer, saying a few words on the side. "To tell you the truth, I don't have any money. I've lived so long, I'm sure it's all gone. Catherine hasn't said so yet, but I expect to hear it any day. What will become of me then, I don't know."

Etta didn't waste any time. Empty pill bottles clattered into wastebaskets. Old magazines and newspapers were stacked up and carried out. Nightgowns were checked, refolded and put back in the drawer. While Etta worked, they talked.

"You don't have no other chirren, just that one girl?"

"That's all. I didn't want any more at the time. My husband did, but I didn't. I should have tried for a boy at least, to carry on the name. What about you?"

"I don't have none at all."

"You didn't want any either?"

"Not unless I was settled down—good husband and all."

"You're not married?"

"That's right."

"No boyfriend?"

"Oh, yeah. I got one of those."

Rose drew a quick half-breath. "I don't guess you could say 'yes, ma'am,' could you? Would that set back the whole Movement?"

The silence that followed was dense with resistance.

"Ah, well," said Rose. "Forget it."

Rose bathed herself sitting up in a chair. In a fresh gown, she watched Etta take away the pan of water and clean up the spills. A bed bath would have been easier on both, but would have cost Rose independence. When Etta had combed and brushed what was left of her hair, she asked for a mirror.

"Time to view the ruins," she said.

Once a day, in a silver mirror with her initials on the back, she looked at herself. As if to hide nothing, she no longer put on make-up. Her hair was drawn back in a thin ponytail. Her face had changed even in shape, had seemed to let go and fall, settling down along the jaw line and pulling everything with it. When she turned her head to the side, she saw jowls. Beneath her chin, loose skin hung like an old stretched sweater. Her eyes, above depressing gray circles, looked out as from a scene of disaster. The eyes themselves, once large and arresting, had shrunk and faded but were still familiar, her lifelong eyes. Her nose too, though thinner and sharper, was the same. Otherwise no trace remained of the vivid girl or dark-haired matron she had been.

All in all, what she saw was a stranger, as much male as female, in whom she was disappearing day by day.

She handed back the mirror in silence.

One morning Rose fixed her eyes on Etta, who was dusting a carved chest of drawers. "You know something?" she said. "The name 'Etta' doesn't suit you. I don't care for that name at all. What if I call you something else, something cute, like Marietta? Or Henrietta?"

Etta shook her head as if humoring a child. "Don't make no nevermind to me."

"You could call me 'Miss Rose.'"

Etta straightened up and turned the dust rag over in her hand. "Naw, I just call you Mrs. Merriweather right on," she said. "That other stuff all over with now."

On the mantle a clock began to strike, its measured strokes tamping down a silence that seemed about to fill the room. Rose drew a deep breath.

"I see," she said. "Then you be Henrietta. Marietta won't do, with Mrs. Merriweather. Too many 'M's.'"

Each day brought new questions and answers.

"How come your phone don't never ring?"

"Out of sight, out of mind, I guess," Rose said, in a moment. "Also, most of my old buddies don't have phones where they are. . . . My daughter calls up sometimes, doesn't she?"

"Yeah, but she times it to when you be sleep, look like."

"That figures."

"You got two grands. They don't never call?"

"Oh, no. They were turned against me years ago, Henrietta. I could be dead, as far as they're concerned."

As if targeted, their questions and answers moved past everdecreasing circles of facts.

"You had just that one husband?"

"Yes, just Allen. A lovely man, a cotton broker." Rose gave a deep sigh. "He deserved better than he got from me. For years I was nothing but a butterfly, just here, there, yonder. A husband and child were the least of my worries. Something finally brought me down, but it was a long time coming, I'm afraid."

Henrietta had stopped pushing the dust mop to listen. She looked at Rose. "You must have kept the house nice, though, and all like that, didn't you?"

"Well, I had a full-time cook and a housemaid. But to answer your question, yes. I did keep it nice. I had a flair for decorating—a 'touch,' people said; and I had something to work with. Furniture from my side of the family, and a collection of silver from Allen's. Big tureens on trays, wine coolers, a writing set. Even a pair of silver peacocks." She smiled, remembering. "The house was lovely, if I do say so, and I looked after it religiously. We polished that silver till it all but put your eyes out. My mother used to say, 'Before you sit down to read your Bible, sweep your front porch.'"

Henrietta was grinning. "Where your Bible at now?"

"Well, where do you want it? Out by my bed for show?"

Henrietta looked down at the mop, moved it absently back and forth. "You pleasured your husband at night, didn't you?"

"Pleasured him?" Rose was taken by surprise. "I guess I did, sometimes."

"You didn't cheat on him, did you?"

She had flirted, Rose thought, with too many; but it was only a game. To test her powers, she supposed. Once, though, it hadn't been flirting, and it hadn't been a game. She didn't answer the question. "I was wild enough, Lord knows," she said, instead. "I was what they called 'fast' back then, a 'fast girl.' Always restless until . . ."

"Unh-uh!" Henrietta interrupted. "Now I know what you was. A flapper!"

Rose laughed. She laughed often now, she'd noticed, and it made her feel good again. At times, almost happy. Dear, sweet Jesus, she thought in the afterglow, please let her stay. Just let her stay till it's over.

The next day she asked for her lap desk and wrote a note to Catherine. "Dear daughter: I like the new nurse you got me very much. She's the best one I've had so far. Please don't let her go without my consent. I'm doing fine now and don't need a thing. Lots of love, Mama." Her writing was large and shaky, but as carefully legible as a second-grade child's.

Then, without warning, she lost a few days. It was like falling asleep at a concert, except that when she woke up the concert was over and everyone had gone.

All but life itself had been stripped away from her. She had no self and no name. Through mental fog she thought of as hell, she had to get back to the bed in which she lay. Across the room, a chest of drawers appeared like someone from the past, someone she ought to know, saying expectantly, "You know me!" She knew nothing. She might have just been born. A blue velvet rocker, with a bathrobe on the back, drew the same kind of blank. Though she shut her eyes tight, tears seeped out and rolled down.

"Look at choo!" The voice was familiar, but she couldn't place it. A hand took hold of hers.

Holding to the hand, Rose opened her eyes. "Oh, God," she said. "God . . ."

The black girl smiled. "You better call on somebody knows you, hadn't you?"

In a flash, the name was back. Henrietta!

"Like who?" Rose said weakly, trying to smile in return. "Who would you suggest?"

Henrietta brought a bowl of homemade soup, a glass of milk, and toast made in the oven. Strengthened, propped up on pillows, Rose waited to hear what had gone on during what she would call, when feeling good, her "temporary demise."

"Your daughter been here," Henrietta said at last. She was sitting in a chair beside the bed.

"Oh? And what did she 'llow?"

"She 'llowed as how we better stop having these spells, or she have to make a change-up."

"Change-up?" Rose looked hard at Henrietta, then lowered her eyes. "Did she say what was wrong with me?"

"It's nothing to say, like I tell you. You comes and goes, and that's it. When you wake up you fine, so quit worrying. Your new style magazine just come. Want to see it?"

"No, thank you."

Henrietta sat on a straight, cane-bottomed chair, a braided wool pad on the seat. Idly, she smoothed the uniform over one compact thigh, then the other. At last she broke the silence.

"Your daughter's not good-looking like you was, is she?"

Rose looked up quickly. "What makes you think I was good-looking?"

"Because you still got them ways. Airish. And your picture bees out, in different rooms."

"It could be my fault she's not more attractive," Rose said. "I was no mother, to anybody. I was out being the belle of the ball myself. I went off and left her with any black woman who'd sleep on a cot in her room. She has every reason to feel the way she does toward me."

The clock struck seven. It was dark outside. Henrietta got up and drew the curtains, then came back to sit by Rose's bed.

"Some chirren come up worse than that," she said, "and don't blame nobody. Besides, she don't have to be stout, and all like that. You didn't give her them weak-sighted eyes. You don't even wear no glasses."

"Do you know what she remembers most about me, as a child?" Rose fixed her eyes on Henrietta. "A few smells, she says. Gardenias from my corsages. Hot cheese in the canapés I served at parties." She looked down. "Chanel Number Five as I went out the door, then alcohol and cigarettes when I came in her room late at night . . ."

Both were silent, thinking.

Henrietta sighed. "She got a pretty face, though. She could get her some contacts, and fix herself up if she wanted to. Unless she don't care. She got a nice husband, like she is."

"Oh, yes. She's a good wife and mother. Very domestic, wonderful cook. Everything I wasn't."

"You fault yourself too much, Mrs. Merriweather. You all right—a nice lady. Everybody make mistakes in life. You ought to see some I have stayed with. Complaining every minute, couldn't please them for nothing. Your folks just don't know how to 'preciate you."

"You didn't know me when I was young, though, Henrietta. 'Spoiled' is not the word."

In the matte blackness of her face, Henrietta's eyes began to twinkle. "You had lots of slaves back then?" she asked.

Rose's eyes twinkled dimly in return. "Ho, ho," she said.

She wasn't feeling jolly underneath. The threat of a "change-up" was still in her mind, like the threat of death itself. Both would be coming soon, she knew. Just not tomorrow or the next day, she hoped.

Breakfast was cantaloupe, cheese grits, little sausages and biscuits. Why so special? Rose wondered. She took her time and enjoyed it all, good food on a pretty tray, thanks in part to Mrs. Fitzhugh Greene, the late Mrs. Fitzhugh Greene. "I was with her till she passed," said Henrietta.

As she leaned over to pour a second cup of coffee, Henrietta delivered the news she'd held back overnight.

"She thinking about selling some stuff out the parlor."

Rose was holding the cup in her hand. She set it carefully back on the table by her bed. "What stuff?"

"Furniture. Mirrors."

Rose waited. "No silver?"

"Just furniture, far as I know, and big gold mirrors. Antique lady coming tomorrow. Not to buy, just look."

Rose said nothing. While Henrietta got things ready for her bath—clean gown, towels, bar of English soap—she stared out the window.

"That's Pardue furniture," she said, at last. "My Grandfather Pardue lived on a plantation and had twelve children. He had that sofa and chairs made in North Carolina for his wife. They shipped it down by boat, my father said." She paused. "As a child, I loved to sit on that sofa and feel the velvet with my hands. I thought all velvet was that faded blue color."

Henrietta brought a pan of hot water and a fresh bath rag. She tested the water with her fingers and flipped them dry over the pan, not touching Rose's towels.

"Tomorrow, you say?" Rose asked. "Could we keep my door shut? I don't want to see her unless I have to."

"You don't have to do nothing. That's how come I'm here."

For the rest of the day Rose was quiet. All afternoon she lay in the darkening room without turning on a reading light. She couldn't eat her supper when it came.

At bedtime Henrietta brought a cup of Ovaltine and sat down by the bed. "Everything be all right," she said, like a spoken lullaby. "She won't do it less she have to, she say. Your money getting low."

"I know," Rose said. "Now run on to bed and let me think."

After breakfast, with Henrietta still in the kitchen, Rose propped herself up in bed without help. When Henrietta came back, she was waiting.

"You know what comes next, don't you?" she asked.

"I'm fixing to cook us some collards. That's what come next. Frost done fell on 'em now, and they'll be good."

"I'll wake up in the nursing home, and you'll be looking for a job."

Henrietta bent down to pick up a pair of bedroom slippers. She placed them neatly by the bed, toes pointing under the mahogany frame.

"We have to be ready, that's all," Rose went on. "So let everything go, and listen. I want you to get something for me out of the bottom of my closet. It's in a round hat box, under an old fur hat. Way back in the back."

She watched Henrietta shoulder her way past dresses on a rod and begin to set out boxes. Boxes of shoes came first: Delman, Amalfi, Bally, I. Miller. Beside them, Henrietta placed a pair of high-heeled black boots. The tops, lightly dusted with mold, flopped over on the floor. There were dated silver sandals, boudoir pillows rewrapped in gift wrappings, purses stuffed with paper to help hold their shapes, and a large pasteboard box labeled "Letters." Finally, Henrietta brought out the hat box and crushed mink hat. Under the hat was a jewelry case of red Chinese brocade.

"She doesn't know about this," Rose said, untying the cord that held the rolled-up case together. From a pocketlike compartment, she took a charm bracelet heavy with charms, gave it a quick look, and laid it on the bed beside her.

Next came a pair of Victorian earrings of thin yellow-gold. She held them up briefly, shook the fancy dangles.

"Mama wore these in the Seminary," she said, and put them down by the bracelet.

When she took out a round baby locket, she paused. "Ah!" She looked at the dented tooth marks, turned the locket over in her hand, tried to remember what was in it. She would open it later and see, she decided, and laid it down by the earrings.

Last she brought out a ring box of faded morocco. Inside, against a background of what was once white satin, a large square sapphire caught the morning light. The stone, of deep but brilliant blue, was surrounded with diamonds like a frame. When it wouldn't go on the ring finger of her arthritic right hand, a hard push got it over the one on her left. On her hand, with its splotches like bruises and navy-blue veins, she looked at the ring and sighed.

"A man not my husband gave me this, years ago." She held out her hand for Henrietta to see. "I never wore it, wasn't supposed to have it; but he said it was the color of my eyes. . . . He wanted me to marry him, leave Allen."

Henrietta sat like a listening child. "You didn't love him?"

"Oh, yes." Rose looked at her. "I love him today, in his grave. But he was married already, with a wife and three children. And I had my own little family. Our paths didn't cross until too late, that's all."

She took off the ring and slipped it back in its slot. Silence fell like an intermission. Overhead, the sound of a plane grew loud, then faded.

"Wear your ring now," said Henrietta.

"No, I want you to give it to Catherine to sell. It could help, a little." She snapped the box shut. "You can tell her I don't know where it came from. Just say I can't remember."

When Henrietta came back with Rose's noon meal, she was smiling. She put down the tray, adjusted Rose's pillows, and set the tray on her lap. Under a metal warming top, beside a slice of ham, was a bowl of collard greens, dark and shiny from the salt pork cooked in them, not too much but not too little for flavor. There was an ear of boiled corn, a crisp brown cornstick, two spring onions, and a small cruet of hot pepper sauce. A sprig of fresh mint bobbed about on top of a glass of iced tea.

Rose looked at the tray. How many times had she sat down to a meal such as this at her own table? From his place at the head, Allen had served the plates. From the foot, she had seen to seconds, refills and bread hot enough to melt butter on contact. For this she had rung a silver bell to the right of her plate. And always, as her mother had taught her, she'd tried to make mealtimes pleasant. "Shoot somebody later," her mother had said.

Looking back, she'd done a few things right, Rose thought. She'd stood by Allen till the end and hadn't faltered. She'd watched him go down year after year, no matter what they did or didn't do, and had braced him up as best she could. Though he couldn't speak at the last, his eyes had lit up when she came into the room. It hadn't all been dancing.

"Thank you, Henrietta," she said. "I don't know when I've had any collards."

"Give you strength," said Henrietta.

Rose ate collards, cornbread, everything, including a piece of pound cake rich with butter and eggs for dessert.

When Henrietta came back for the tray, Rose asked her to sit.

"How long before I 'goes' again, do you think?" she asked.

Henrietta was slow to answer. "Can't nobody tell about that," she said.

"What will become of you?"

"I be taking care of somebody right on. I don't have no trouble finding jobs."

They sat in silence, looking out the window.

"You never told me what you want in this world," Rose said at last. "I'd like to know before we part."

"What I want?" Henrietta frowned. "My mama told me to don't want nothing, just take what God send and be thankful." She stood up and took the tray. "Sometime He send a little satisfaction along. I be looking out for that."

Rose propped up on an elbow. "That's what you've been to me," she cried, staring at Henrietta with wide naked eyes. "A satisfaction!" She opened her mouth to say more, but something closed in her throat.

On the tray, dishes began to slide and Henrietta had to stop them. "Nap time," she said quickly, with everything back in place.

Rose watched her leave the room, heard her rubber soles squeak down the hall. The kitchen door swung open and shut.

Rose made her way to the edge of the bed. Careful not to lose her balance, she opened the drawer to the table beside it and took out the jewelry case there.

Inside the locket there was nothing. No picture, no baby hair, nothing. As it lay on her palm, she could hear again a fat girl sobbing, bubbles on her braces. "Leave me alone, Mama! You don't care about me. All you want is for me to be alive." And later, the same girl, older and calmer but the same. "Why can't you understand, Mama? I don't want to wear your wedding dress. If Jesus came down and made it fit me, I still wouldn't wear it."

Briefly, Rose looked over the charms on the bracelet. One of her father's cuff links; a gold cross from her grandmother Rose—Rose Lanier St. Clair, she was, a model of virtue but plain; a round disc engraved in old-fashioned script—Rose Pardue, Black Belt Cotton Queen, 1917; an eighteen-karat gold number "1."

Carefully, she put it all back in the drawer.

Stretched out at last, flat on her back except for her head on a pillow, she turned her face toward the window and thought of the blank from which she'd so far returned. A long shudder possessed her. She fought it off with a full deep breath, which she let out by degrees, and fixed her mind on the ring, the furniture, and a possible happy ending. The ring could save the furniture, Catherine could somehow forgive her, then she could forgive herself, and so on.

She didn't hear the doorbell when the antique dealer came, nor Henrietta hurrying down the hall to let her in.

When, on their way to the parlor, Henrietta looked in before closing the door, Rose was asleep. Pale, thin, neatly covered by the bedspread, she was almost like a wrinkle on the big Pardue bed, something a hand could smooth out.

$\mathscr{C}$ Once in a Lifetime

HER NAME WAS EDITH, but in junior high school she'd changed the spelling to Edythe. She dotted her i's with small circles and used them for periods. Notes she passed to boys in the hall were thick with underlined words, quotation marks, and exclamation points. At the end of certain sentences she wrote "Ha-Ha."

She had regular features and thick shoulder-length hair the color of peanut brittle. Her eyes and lightly suntanned skin glowed with health. Though she wore dresses made at home and no makeup or jewelry, other girls looked at her with envy. Sitting at her desk she appeared bored and sleepy, but out of class she was lively and sociable, good at athletics. She liked attention, even teasing, which she took with good humor.

Everyone liked her, but she was hardly noticed in the town until she was past thirty, divorced, and the mother of a teen-age daughter. Married at eighteen, she'd lived twenty miles in the country with an alcoholic husband, so abusive that she and the child had spent more than one winter night hiding in the woods, huddled up in quilts. When he finally left her for another woman she came back to town, thin and subdued. In September, she went to work as a waitress at Spiro's Cafe. The year was 1950.

As she gained back lost weight, she became her old self again, almost. She carried large trays of dishes with the same zest she'd once dribbled a basketball. Waiting on people, seeing them eat, seemed to make her happy.

"Anything wrong?" she'd ask, seeing a displeased expression or pushed-back plate. "Want me to take it back?"

Mr. Spiro stopped having the usual complaints and mix-ups on orders, and raised her salary before Christmas. Nearly everyone left a nice tip.

In one way, though, she'd changed. She no longer liked attention and even tried to avoid it. With her face bare of makeup and hair pulled back tight to thwart the curl, she smiled as before but had little to say.

Each day, when the noon rush was over, she had a few minutes free. She'd go up front alone and sit on a stool by the cash register, staring out the window as if lost in a daydream, oblivious to anyone who saw her and waved from outside.

While she was at work, her daughter, Denise Louise, was in school or at home, in the large room and kitchen they rented from an elderly widow who wanted someone in the house for protection. Sometimes, too, Denise Louise was on the street. In a group she was always on the fringes. Alone, she walked close to store windows, studying the displays and herself at the same time. Dark like her father, she was well developed, with a round face and sharp black eyes.

At night she ate with Edythe in the cafe, where she waited in a back booth until her mother was through. Then Edythe brought their served plates and they ate across from each other, sometimes talking, sometimes not. When Edythe looked at Denise, it was the way a mother cow looks at her calf, as if a warm mother tongue might come out and lick at any moment. When they'd eaten, Edythe would hurriedly clean off the table and get her purse. They then walked home together side by side, walking fast, sometimes arm in arm.

One morning, as if to make a happy announcement, Mr. Spiro's wife brought in a vase of early jonquils picked from her yard. She placed it up front by the cash register for everyone to see and enjoy. The day was mild and Edythe wore no sweater. Customers, ready for spring, seemed more cheerful.

And that was the morning Stanhope Rogers came in. Usually, he patronized a truck stop on the highway, Edythe found out later, but today he'd brought a load of calves to the stockyard. They'd sold, and his next stop would be the bank. He'd dropped by Spiro's for a cup of coffee.

When Edythe took his order, he turned sideways in the booth to look at her. "Didn't I go to school with you a hundred years ago?" he said. "Ain't your name. . . Edythe?"

Edythe smiled. "I didn't think you'd remember me, Stanhope."

"Remember?" A grin melted slowly over Stanhope's face. "I never forgot you, Edie."

Stanhope was the only son of the town's most prosperous (some said slickest) lawyer. A lifelong rebel, he'd refused to finish high school. He affected a poor-boy lack of polish that managed to poke fun at his background without real disrespect. "That Stanhope!" people would say, glad to see him on the street in work clothes, or in a tux at a country club dance. His job was looking after his father's land and cattle, which everyone assumed would someday be his. At thirty-six, he'd dated most of the girls near his age in the town, without coming close to marriage. "Too scared!" he'd say, when kidded.

When Edythe brought his coffee, he looked at her again. "How you been gettin along all this time, Edie?"

"Just fine, Stanhope."

"Didn't you get married?"

"Yeah. I didn't graduate with the rest."

"You and me." He struck a match with his thumnbnail and lit a cigarette. "Your husband here in town?"

"No, I'm divorced now."

"I see. Any kids?"

"Just one girl. She's with me."

Mr. Spiro had other waitresses, one and sometimes two, but

Edythe was always busy with no time to chat. When Stanhope went up front to pay his check, though, she swerved up with an arm full of dishes.

"You come back, Stanhope," she said, and smiled. She couldn't believe he'd remembered her name.

"I'll do that little thing, Edie," he said, and took his cowboy hat from the coat rack.

When she cleaned off his table, she found an uncalled-for tip.

In school all the girls had been stuck on Stanhope, she remembered. She had too, but from such a distance it didn't count. He was from a different world, a world she knew nothing about. And now she had no interest in men from any world. Free of her husband, she was satisfied with her job and her child. Her one goal was to give Denise what she thought of as a chance in life.

The next time Stanhope came in, it was five o'clock in the afternoon. And he came for a meal.

"My nigger cook is out sick today, and I don't feel like cooking," he told Edythe when she brought a menu, which he waved aside. "What you got?"

"You want a steak?"

"If it's good." He gave her a teasing look. "Make it medium."

She told the cook twice, a good steak, medium. But when she brought it out, it looked underdone and she made a point of checking back when he cut into it.

"Why, that's rare!"

He grinned. "Yep. I've seen 'em hurt worse than this and get well."

"I'll take it back! Won't take but a minute. I'm sorry, Stanhope!"

But he was already chewing. "This is the way I like it, Edie. In a country cafe, you tell 'em medium and you get rare every time. Rare's what I wanted."

She didn't know whether to believe him or not, but she kept his coffee hot and brought homemade rolls heated up from noon. They had good apple pie and he took it a la mode.

When he was through, he came back to where she was tending the coffee urn.

"Just between you and me, Edie, that steak was tough. But I liked the service."

"Well, thanks, Stanhope. You come back."

That night in bed (Edythe slept with Denise in an iron double bed painted white) she found herself thinking about Stanhope. How had he managed to stay single so long? He was better-looking now than when they were in school. And he'd always been sweet, not at all stuck up. Some girl would be lucky to get him, she thought. She sighed and turned over again.

"Do your feet hurt, Mama?" Denise asked in the dark.

"Why, baby, I thought you were asleep! No, my feet don't hurt."

"If they have that class party, Mama, we're supposed to wear evening dresses. Where will I get an evening dress?"

"We'll have to start saving up."

"Can we save up enough?"

"Why, sure we can."

"For a long dress, off the shoulder, with a stiff petticoat?"

"I hope to tell you! Now you go to sleep."

The town was so quiet it might have disappeared in the darkness. Except for Denise, Edythe felt alone in an unfolding mystery, sometimes kind, more often cruel. How much would an evening dress cost, and how would she pay for it? She couldn't go to sleep, but didn't want to move and disturb Denise.

Near their bed a window was up, and the fresh scent of a Breath of Spring bush, in full bloom, reached her. It brought a comforting thought. That bush had been through hard winters too, and here it was, blooming again. The next thing she knew it was morning.

Stanhope came back sooner than she expected. He wore his work clothes as usual, but this time he seemed more business-like.

"Hello, Edie," he said. "Coffee, please, ma'am."

He had something on his mind, she could tell. So she said nothing and hurried up his order.

When she set the cup before him, he didn't look up at first. "What are you doing tonight, Miss Edie?" he asked.

"What do you mean, what am I doing?"

"I want you to have supper with me, for a change. How about it?"

"But I don't get off till after supper!"

"Whose supper?" He grinned at her. "I'll pick you up at eight o'clock. Okay?"

Her answer was almost involuntary. It came out like a breath. "Well all right, I guess, Stanhope. . ."

He was gone by the time she realized what she'd done. Had she lost her mind completely? She hadn't even asked where he would pick her up. Did he know where she lived, and would he come there for the old lady to see and talk about? The most important thing was how Denise would take it.

But Denise was more excited than she was. Never before in her life had either of them had a date.

"You mean Mr. Rogers, that rich man?"

Well, it's his Daddy that's rich, not him. You sure you won't be scared?"

Denise's sharp eyes were serious. "Scared of what?"

Stanhope apparently understood about the old lady. Right on time his car drove up, but stopped slightly beyond the house. Edythe, dressed and ready, and Denise in pajamas, were peeping through the blinds as he got out, lit a cigarette, and waited as in a scene from a movie. Edythe hugged Denise.

"Bye, baby. Go to bed early."

"I will, Mama. Bye."

Edythe checked the night latch, carefully closed the door, and hurried across the lawn.

"Hello, girl." Stanhope helped her in and shut the door.

He had not dressed up as she had, but wore clean khakis. He took her straight to what he called "the cabin," five miles in the country, where he lived alone. Batched, as he called it. The cabin was a camp house with combination living-eating room, two bedrooms, a bathroom and kitchen. He led Edythe in as though she'd been there before, straight to the kitchen, where a hanging light bulb glared on two large steaks, a black iron skillet, and a bottle of bourbon.

"Not for me, Stanhope," she said, when he began filling the second fruit juice glass with bourbon.

"Why not?"

"I don't know. I just never do."

He drank his, chased it with water, and downed what he'd poured into her glass before she stopped him. He smacked his lips, said "Aaah," and handed her a man-sized apron. Then they worked in silence, cutting up and frying potatoes, making a salad of vegetables fresh from his garden. Outside a whippoorwill gave its strangled, lonely cry. From time to time a pointer, knowing his master was there, scratched at the door.

"Let him in," Edythe said.

"Not now," he said. "Time to eat." He rubbed the hot skillet with a piece of sizzling fat, and dropped in the steaks.

They ate from a table covered with red-checked oilcloth, centered with bottles of catsup and Worcestershire sauce. His salt and pepper shakers were aluminum kitchenware, extra large.

"Watch out for that salt," he warned. "It don't fool around coming out."

Since it was late, they were hungry and ate fast, cleaning their plates. But when Edythe stood up to clear the table, he held up his hand.

"No, ma'am. We've done our do in here," he said, and snapped off the light.

But in the living room, Edythe became suddenly self-conscious. She chose an overstuffed chair by a table covered with magazines and Extension Service bulletins. She picked up a *Progressive Farmer* and began leafing through it.

"We tried to farm out there, for a while," she said, and shook her head.

Stanhope watched her from the sofa. "Come over here, Edie," he said, and smiled.

When she didn't move, he got up and led her by the hand. He put his arm around her, leaned his head against hers, and patted her arm. When he kissed her it was sweetly, the way he smiled.

"I like you, Edie," he said. "You're the most beautiful woman I ever saw in my life, and you don't even know it!" Then he started to kiss her seriously.

Gently, she drew away. "I like you too, Stanhope," she said in a headlong voice. "But I'm on my own now. I have to go straight . . ."

The next morning when Denise, who'd been sleeping soundly when Edythe came in, asked what kind of time she had, Edythe said it was nice, a good supper. She was cooking breakfast as usual before going to work, and she didn't look up from the skillet. Denise asked no more, as if she knew without details that things hadn't worked out quite storybook style.

Edythe didn't expect to see Stanhope again, but he was back within the week, to take her to a movie in a neighboring town. After that, she went back to the cabin several times, once with Denise along at his insistence. They began going to a nearby drive-in movie, and one night drove sixty miles to the city for a meal. Edythe was in love with him from the start, but summer was almost over before they were lovers.

Afterward she saw him regularly on Sunday nights, then on Sunday and Wednesday nights, and sometimes in between. Since she worried about Denise at home alone, he had a phone put in her room so that Denise could reach them at the cabin. Then he began to call every night around eight.

"Anything going on?"

"Not really. Kiwanis Club lunch today."

"Lord God. I forgot all about it."

"So I noticed." She laughed.

"I got a little something done out here, though. Fixed that fence that needed fixing." The land and cattle were his main interest, Edythe had learned within a week. Maybe his first love as well.

Their nightly conversations were brief but charged with intimacy.

"You all right, then?"

"Fine. How about you?"

"Fine. Sure. Well, goodnight, hon."

Each time he called her 'hon' Edythe was shot through with the exact opposite of a pain, for which she knew no word. But over the phone she was careful of what she said, because Denise was there listening, at least in the beginning.

Soon after the class party, to which she wore her new dress (Stanhope had put the money in Edythe's purse and wouldn't take it back), Denise began to have dates of her own. At first she went to Sunday matinees or early shows on Friday nights, but with the coming of fall she had so many invitations Edythe had to call a halt.

"No," she found herself saying, time after time. "No, ma'am!"

The boys Denise attracted were older boys, boys with cars and part-time jobs, money to spend.

"But why?" Denise asked furiously. "You just don't want me to have any fun!"

"I want you to have fun, but you'll have plenty of time for boys later on. What you need to do now is get through school, and try to be somebody."

"You didn't get through school."

"No. And look at me now!"

Arguing didn't help and Denise's resentment seemed to grow. She stopped saying "But I'm fifteen now" and "All the other girls do," and listened in silence, eyes hard as agates.

"I guess I ought not to see you so much, Stanhope," Edythe told him one night, coming back from the cabin.

"Been listening to the gossips?"

"No," she said. "It's Denise."

Absorbed as she was with Stanhope and Denise, Edythe hadn't been concerned about how their relationship was perceived in the town. She had noticed that when she approached a table at work, conversations sometimes broke off and people looked embarrassed. Once she'd heard an outburst of laughter before she was out of hearing. Now and then she found someone staring at her curiously. But she would have needed more conceit to realize that she, Stanhope, and Denise were now the talk of the town.

Then, for no reason, her problem with Denise seemed to solve itself, in a way. Denise stopped asking to go out at all. At the same time she withdrew, like an enemy defeated in battle but still at all-out war. When Edythe left at night with Stanhope, she would be studying, washing her hair, or doing her nails. Her grades had gone down, but not below C. She was bright, very bright, her homeroom teacher had told Edythe in the cafe one day, a straight-A student if she applied herself.

When school was out, Denise got a job at the dime store to help pay for books and clothes in the fall. And though they roomed together, ate together, and shared a bed at night, Edythe felt that she now lived with a stranger, someone who carried on her real existence elsewhere.

Late in July Edythe, who was never sick, caught a cold that was severe. By Friday night when she went to the cabin with Stanhope, she had a headache and ached all over. When she couldn't eat, Stanhope put his hand on her forehead and decided she had fever.

"I better get you back before the drug store closes," he said. "You need medicine."

So it was nine-thirty instead of twelve when Edythe unlocked the door and let herself in. By the bathroom light, the room was semi-dark as usual and she made no noise so as not to wake Denise. Stanhope had gone by the time she realized that Denise was not in bed, not in the apartment at all. She turned on every light, looked stupidly in the kitchen and back again, unable to believe it.

Convinced at last, she sat on the bed, shivering in the hot night, trying to think what to do. She could call the police, but then people would know. That Denise was out with a boy, she was sure. But what boy, and how many times it had happened before, she had no idea. The last few months were now bitterly explained.

Alternately, she walked from room to room and stood looking out through the blinds. Twice she went to the phone to call Stanhope but decided against it. Passing the dresser she caught a glimpse of her white, distraught face, and made herself lie down. No sooner had she stretched out than she remembered the medicine they'd bought, and got up to take it. At eleven-thirty she heard a key in the lock.

Denise was taken aback only for a second. She closed the door, walked to the dresser and put down the small clutch bag she carried.

"You're back early," she said to Edythe, now up in her stocking feet, still in her clothes.

"Where have you been?" Edythe caught Denise by the shoulders and shook her, searching her face, as if the answer were to be seen, not heard.

"Where have you been, Mama?"

The question seemed to hang intact between them, growing larger, growing monstrous. Edythe backed away as if she'd been slapped.

Denise began undressing as on any other night. She hung up her dress, placed her low-heeled slippers side by side on the closet floor, and put on her pajamas. Without a word, she got into bed and pulled up the sheet.

At last Edythe got in beside her, as far on her side as possible. They lay darkly awake, side by side, until Edythe knew, by her breathing, that Denise was asleep.

Edythe didn't sleep at all. Before daylight, she got up and turned off the alarm clock. Her cold had been shocked into the background, it seemed, but she took the medicine for whatever comfort it might bring. Then she dressed and cooked breakfast as usual, but left it on the stove. Since it was Saturday, she didn't wake Denise.

At the cafe, Mr. Spiro noticed her pale face and dark-circled eyes. "You all right, Miss Edythe?"

"Yes, sir. It's just a cold."

But at twelve-thirty she stole a minute from the noon rush to call Stanhope. He was always at the cabin in the middle of the day.

"Don't call tonight," she said in a low voice, directly into the receiver so that no one could hear. "I'll call you when I can."

"Something wrong?"

"Yes, but I can't talk now. I'm at work."

"All right, hon." He let her go.

But immediately following the noon exodus, he walked into the cafe, casually, as if happening by. He stopped up front to buy a pack of cigarettes from Mr. Spiro.

"I'd like to borrow Miss Edythe for a few minutes," he said, as he picked up his change. "I'll get her right back."

"Take her," Mr. Spiro said. "And don't hurry. She's sick." From the start, it had been obvious that Mr. Spiro liked Stanhope, liked for Edythe to be with him.

To Edythe, Stanhope said simply, "Let's go."

Outside, he took her arm and guided her to his car. As they walked, she kept her head down like a criminal before cameras. In the car, he said nothing until they were on the outskirts of town.

"Now," he said evenly. "What's wrong?"

She told him what had happened, and all that had been said.

"So I know what I have to do." She took a deep breath. "I have to stop seeing you, Stanhope. I've got to get her straightened out, if I can."

Driving slowly, he'd listened in silence. Now he pulled over to the side of the country road and stopped. He turned to Edythe, extended his arm across the back of the seat, and smiled as upon a small, everyday problem.

"Well," he said. "I guess it's time we got married."

"Got married. . . ?"

"Give me a little time to break it to my folks. They're liable to raise Cain, but go ahead and tell Denise. Tell her we'll try to make her a nice home."

There were things in life that Edythe had always accepted as out of her reach. Being Stanhope's wife was one of those things. She'd expected nothing from him, except to be with him as long as it pleased him. Now he said they should be married! His own idea. In spite of everything, something inside her began to fizz up with a joy she'd never felt before.

She was back at work in less than an hour and, without a word to anyone, began trying to make up for lost time.

Denise didn't come in for supper, so Edythe had an order of fried chicken fixed up to take home. After work, she hurried through the dusk, walking fast, wondering if Denise would be there, and what she would do if she weren't. With her hand on the doorknob, she took a deep breath before she turned it.

Denise sat at a table that served as study desk in winter. She was putting on nail polish by the light of a crook-necked lamp. She wore shorts and no make-up, and to Edythe her face was childlike still.

"I brought you something to eat." She put the food on a corner of the table.

Denise finished one hand and held it up for the polish to dry. "Good," she said.

Across the street, children of the neighborhood were getting in their last minutes of outdoor play. Their high-pitched voices came through the window as from a lost world of innocence. Edythe took a straight chair near the table. She longed to take off her shoes and rest her tired feet, but felt it would detract from whatever dignity she had left.

"Denise," she said quickly. "We'll forget about last night, but don't think it will happen again—because it won't. From now on, I'm going to be here."

Denise looked her in the eye, with what Edythe took for contempt.

"It was my fault, for ever leaving you in the first place," she went on. "But maybe it wasn't as bad as it looked. Mr. Rogers is going to marry me."

"Marry you?"

"He told me to tell you we'll try to make you a nice home."

Denise said nothing for a moment. "When is all this coming off?"

"After he tells his folks."

"Oh, I see. That may take a while."

Denise uncovered the food, picked out a piece of chicken, and began to eat. Edythe took off her shoes and flexed her tired toes. By nine o'clock their lights were out.

The next night, when Edythe and Denise came out of the cafe to go home, Stanhope was waiting in his car. He helped Denise in first, to the middle of the front seat, then Edythe.

"I thought you girls might like a little fresh air," he said, paying special attention to Denise, who had never said much more than yes, sir and no, sir, in his presence.

He drove by the high school, the swimming pool and ball park, then home where he stopped but made no move to get out. Instead he reached across to the glove compartment and took out a small gift-wrapped package, which he handed to Denise.

"A little something for your mother," he said. "Open it for her, sugar."

With careful fingers, Denise removed the wrapping from a jeweler's ring box and turned, wide-eyed, to Edythe.

"You open it," Edythe whispered.

A solitaire in a Tiffany setting caught the light of the dashboard and flung it about.

"Oh!" Denise and Edythe said, together.

Denise thrust the box at her mother, whose hands trembled as she took it.

"Well, see if it fits!" Stanhope prompted.

Edythe slipped it on her ring finger and, half-laughing, half-crying, held up her hand.

She wore the ring to work as Stanhope told her. No one could miss it. Several people picked up her hand and admired it, but no one had the nerve to say, "What does it mean?" Edythe gave no explanation. Only when she happened to be in the rest room alone, she held up her hand and looked at it as at some recently acquired, glorified part, perhaps a wing.

As weeks went by, she didn't ask Stanhope if he'd told his parents, or when the date might be. But she didn't go out with him either, except for daytime outings with Denise always along.

Finally one day, Denise said, "You don't have to keep staying here with me, Mama. I'm not going anywhere." She lowered her eyelids and sighed. "I don't have any place to go."

At night Edythe noticed that she sat with books open before her, but seldom turned the pages. Sometimes she turned pages too fast, as if scanning. She'd grown quiet, not so much dutiful as sad. Several times when Edythe was at home, the phone rang and she turned down invitations without even asking for permission.

"I don't want you to stay here all the time, baby," Edythe told her. "I just want to know where you are, and that you're with a nice boy."

"Oh, I know . . . "

One day Edythe opened the door when Denise wasn't expecting her. She was talking to someone on the phone with urgency in her voice. When she saw Edythe, she hung up abruptly without saying goodbye. And though she hurried to the bathroom and began washing out underwear she'd put in soak, Edythe saw that she'd been crying.

She pretended not to notice, but something hidden had almost been revealed. From then on, she was more watchful, and more worried.

When Denise brought home the news from school that Mr. Rogers had indeed told his parents and that they were having a duck fit, Edythe knew that she told her out of loyalty, not spite.

"They say they're going to cut him off without a cent," she reported. "Maybe not even let him run the place any more."

For Stanhope's birthday they worked together, late into the night, baking a cake. Denise got the recipe from her home economics teacher and directed each step. It was she who read, measured, and decided what to do next, while Edythe followed directions and did the heavy beating. As they worked, Edythe felt that they were friends again as before. Moreover, finished and frosted, the cake was fine. For all her concerns and uncertainties, Edythe went to bed happy.

When, the next morning, she heard Denise sick in the bathroom, the suspicion that rose like a flushed covey of quail in her brain seemed so preposterous she disowned it at once. Denise was only sixteen, a junior in high school. She wasn't even going steady.

"You did too much tasting last night," she said.

But when Denise was sick again the following morning, she knew at once that she'd really known the first time, or even before that. Perhaps she'd always known that things would turn out something like this for both of them.

She put her arms around Denise and let her cry. Fall had arrived, not with burnt orange and winey air this year, but grey skies and mists of rain. In the drab early morning, with her daughter's head on her shoulder, Edythe stared dry-eyed before her, the way she'd once seen a country neighbor stand and watch her house burn down, its glowing rafters collapsing at last into the heart of the flames.

"Mama will stand by you," she said, and tightened her arms. "Do you know who's to blame?"

Denise shook her head and sobbed harder. Then she pulled away to face her mother with wet, contorted face.

"Me!" she sobbed. "I'm the one to blame. Oh, mama, mama, what will we do?"

"We'll do the best we can," Edythe said. "That's all we can do."

It was two days before she saw Stanhope. When he called at night, she said the usual things, except that her voice was so sad, so full of tenderness, he hesitated before hanging up.

When he said, "Could you get away Sunday night, just for a little while?" she said yes, she could.

She washed her hair and wore it loose for a change, put on a full skirt and peasant-type blouse that Stanhope liked. When she told Denise goodbye, it was Denise whose eyes wavered, not hers.

Stanhope had changed. Trouble did not become him. His eyes seemed not so much blue as grey, like overcast skies.

"We might as well pick a day, Edie," he said. "I can't win my folks over, and I've given up trying. We'll be strapped at first, but I've been asking around about jobs. . . " There was a brief flash of his old light spirit. "You weren't marrying me for my money, were you?"

Later, that was as far as Edythe let herself remember, most of the time. Not that the rest was less dear. She'd told him that it had to end anyway, and then she told him why. If he suggested getting rid of it, it was no more than she'd considered already, she and Denise together. The arguments he brought up were the same they'd used at home, over and over.

"No," she said, finally. "We've decided to go through with it, I guess."

That he would have gone through it with them if she'd let him, she had no doubt. That he would have lived to regret it, she was reasonably sure.

On a rainy night in the dead of winter, she and Denise went to the hospital in a taxi. The baby was a girl. Denise wanted to name her for Edythe, but Edythe wouldn't have it. "Let's get her a name from the Bible," she said. "Maybe it will help her." They decided on Martha.

During Denise's two-week confinement, no one sent a flower, gift, or card, except Mr. and Mrs. Spiro. No one came to see the baby except a Roman Catholic priest who also visited criminals in jail, people said.

But in time life took up where it had left off. Even disgrace wears thin, wears out, and begins to fade like glory. Denise found a job in a dress shop and paid an older woman to look after Martha in the daytime. At night she and Edythe tried to make it up to her.

In the dress shop, Denise became indispensable, able to support herself and Martha until she met and married an electrician from a neighboring town. He was a good man and a good provider. Soon after the marriage he adopted Martha, and treated her as he treated the two children of his own that Denise gave him.

With time running out, Stanhope married too, after a while. He married an acceptable girl, who'd been away teaching school at the time of his "affair." Afterwards he drank too much and put on weight, but fathered two children. He finally settled down, people said. The cabin grew up in weeds and vines, and no one went there any more.

Only for Edythe, nothing seemed to change. She worked the

same long hours at the cafe as before. At night she went back to her one room and kitchen, where Denise usually called before bedtime.

Her face was like a good piece of sculpture to which the artist returned year after year, deepening a line, smoothing an angle, but always for the better. At the cafe, when she had a few minutes to spare, she still went up front and sat on the stool to look out the window. Her expression, though, was different. Her gaze was no longer dreamy but thoughtful. In her eyes there were no regrets.

A New Life

THEY MEET BY CHANCE in front of the bank. Elizabeth is a recent widow, pale and dry-eyed, unable to cry. Paul, an old friend, old boyfriend, starts smiling the moment he sees her. He looks so happy, she thinks. She's never seen him look so happy. Under one arm he carries a wide farm checkbook, a rubber band around it so things won't fall out.

"Well. This is providential." He grips her hand and holds on, beaming, ignoring the distance he's long kept between them. Everything about him seems animated. Even his hair, thick, dark, shot with early gray, stands up slightly from his head instead of lying down flat. In the sunlight the gray looks electric. "We've been thinking about you," he says, still beaming. "Should have been to see you."

"But you did come." Something about him is different, she thinks, something major, not just the weight he's put on.

"We came when everyone else was there and you didn't need us. We should have been back long ago. How are you?"

"Fine," she says, to end it. "Thank you."

He studies her face, frowns. "You don't look fine," he says.

"You're still grieving, when John is with God now. He's well again. Happy! Don't you know that?"

So that's it, she thinks. She's heard that Paul and his wife, Louise, are in a new religious group in town, something that has sprung up outside the church. They call themselves Keepers of the Vineyard. Like a rock band, someone said.

Small-town traffic moves up and down the street, a variety of mid-size cars and pickup trucks, plus an occasional big car or van. The newly remodeled bank updates a street of old red-brick buildings, some now painted white, green, gray. Around the corner the beauty shop is pink with white trim.

This is the southern Bible Belt, where people talk about God the way they talk about the weather, about His will and His blessings, about why He lets things happen. The Vineyard people claim that God also talks to them. Their meeting place is a small house on Green Street, where they meet, the neighbors say, all the time. Night and day.

Their leader is the new young pastor of the Presbyterian church, called by his first name, Steve. Regular church members look on the group with suspicion. They're all crazy, they go too far, the church people say.

When told, Steve had simply shrugged. "Some thought Jesus was a little crazy, too," he'd said.

He is a spellbinding preacher and no one moves or dozes while he speaks, but his church is split in two. Some are for him and some against him, but none are neutral. He is defined by extremes.

Paul opens the door to the bank for Elizabeth. "What are you doing tonight?" he asks, over her shoulder.

She looks back, surprised, and he winks.

"Louise and I could come over after supper," he says. "How about it?"

She understands his winks and jokes. They're coverup devices, she'd discovered years ago, for all he meant to hide. New hurts, old wounds, the real Paul Dudley. Only once had she seen him show pain, ever. After his favorite dog, always with him, had been hit by a truck, he'd covered his face with his hands when he told her. But the minute she'd touched him, ready to cry too, he'd stiffened. "I'll have to get another one," he'd said. And right away, he had. Another lemon-spotted pointer.

"You're turning down a good way of life, though," her mother had said, a little sadly, when she didn't take the ring. It had been his mother's diamond. He'd also inherited a large tract of land and a home in the country.

She'd never confessed one of her reasons, for fear that it might sound trivial. He'd simply made her nervous. Wherever they'd gone, to concerts, plays, movies, he hadn't been able to sit still and listen, but had had to look around and whisper, start conversations, pick up dropped programs. Go for more popcorn. He had rummaged through his hair, fiddled with his tie, jiggled keys in his pocket until it had been all she could do not to say, "Stop that, or I'll scream!"

He hadn't seemed surprised when she told him. Subdued at first, he had rallied and joked as he went out the door. But he'd cut her out of his life from then on, and ignored all her efforts to be friendly. Not until both were married, to other people, had he even stopped on the street to say hello.

Back home now in her clean, orderly kitchen, she has put away groceries and stored the empty bags. Without putting it off, she has subtracted the checks she'd just written downtown. Attention to detail has become compulsive with her. It is all that holds her together, she thinks.

Just before daylight-savings dark, Paul and Louise drive up in a white station wagon. Paul is wearing a fresh short-sleeved shirt, the tops of its sleeves still pressed together like uncut pages in a book. In one hand he carries a Bible as worn as a wallet.

Louise, in her late forties like Elizabeth, is small and blonde. Abandoned first by a father who had simply left home, then by a mother his leaving had destroyed, she'd been brought up by sad, tired grandparents. Her eyes are like those of an unspoiled pet, waiting for a sign to be friendly.

When Elizabeth asks if they'd like something to drink now or later, they laugh. It's a long-standing joke around Wakefield. "Mr. Paul don't drink nothing but sweetmilk," a worker on his place had said years ago.

"Now would be nice," he says, with his happy new smile.

Elizabeth leads the way to a table in her kitchen, a large light room with one end for dining. The table, of white wood with an airy glass top, overlooks her back lawn. While she fills glasses with tea and ice, Paul gazes out the window, humming to himself, drumming on the glass top. Louise admires the marigolds, snapdragons, and petunias in bloom. Her own flowers have been neglected this year, she says. Elizabeth brings out a pound cake still warm from the oven.

"Let's bless it," Paul says, when they're seated.

He holds out one hand to her and the other to Louise. His hand is trembling and so warm it feels feverish. Because of her?, Elizabeth thinks. No. Everyone knows he's been happy with his wife. Louise's hand is cool and steady.

He bows his head. "Lord, we thank you for this opportunity to witness in your name. We know that You alone can comfort our friend in her sorrow. Bring her, we pray, to the knowledge of your saving grace and give her your peace, which passes understanding. We ask it for your sake and in your name."

He smiles a benediction, and Elizabeth cuts the cake.

"The reason we're here, Elizabeth—" He pushes back the tea and cake before him, "—is that my heart went out to you this morning at the bank. You can't give John up, and it's tearing you apart."

What can she say? He's right. She can't give John up and she is torn apart, after more than a year.

"We have the cure for broken hearts," he says, as if stating a fact.

Louise takes a bite of cake, but when he doesn't she puts down her fork. On her left hand, guarded by the wedding band, is a ring that Elizabeth remembers.

"I have something to ask you, Elizabeth." Paul looks at her directly. "Are you saved?"

Elizabeth turns her tea glass slowly clockwise, wipes up the circle beneath it with her napkin. "I don't know how to answer that, Paul," she says, at last. "What happened to John did something to my faith. John didn't deserve all that suffering, or to die in his prime. I can't seem to accept it."

"Well, that's natural. Understandable. In my heart I was rebellious too, at one time."

She frowns, trying to follow. He hadn't been religious at all when she'd known him. On the contrary, he'd worked on a tractor all day Sunday while everyone else went to church, had joked about people who were overly religious.

"But I had an encounter with Jesus Christ that changed my life," he says. "I kept praying, with all my heart, and He finally came to me. His presence was as real as yours is now!" His eyes fill up, remembering. "But you have to really want Him, first. Most people have to hit rock bottom, the way I did, before they do. You have to be down so low you say, 'Lord, I can't make it on my own. You'll have to help me. You take over!'"

Now he's lost her. Things had gone so well for him, she'd thought. He'd had everything he said he wanted out of life when they were dating— a big family, and to live on his land. He'd been an only child whose parents had died young. Louise had been orphaned too, in a way. So they'd had a child every year or two before they quit, a station wagon full of healthy, suntanned children. Some were driving themselves by now, she'd noticed.

As for her, rock bottom had been back in that hospital room with John, sitting in a chair by his bed. Six months maybe, a year at the most, they'd just told her out in the hall. She'd held his hand until the Demerol took effect and his hand had gone limp in hers. Then she'd leaned her head on the bed beside him and prayed, with all her heart. From hospital room to hospital room she had prayed, and at home in between.

"I've said that too, Paul, many times," she says. "I prayed, and nothing happened. Why would He come to you and not me?"

"Because you were letting something stand in the way, my dear!" His smile is back, full force. "For Him to come in, you have to get rid of self—first of all your self-will ! 'Not my will but Thine be done,' He said on the cross."

He breaks off, takes a quick sip of tea. With the first bite of cake, he shuts his eyes tight. A blissful smile melts over his face.

"Umh, umh!" He winks at Louise. "How about this pound cake, Mama!"

Late the next afternoon, Elizabeth is watering flowers in her back yard. Before, she grew flowers to bring in the house, zinnias for pottery pitchers, bulbs for clear glass vases. Now she grows them for themselves, and seldom cuts them. She has a new irrational notion that scissors hurt the stems. After what she's seen of pain, she wants to hurt nothing that lives.

From where she stands with the hose, she sees a small red car turn into her driveway. In front of the house, two young girls in sundresses get out.

"Mrs. North?" the first girl says, when Elizabeth comes up to meet them. "You probably don't remember me, but I'm Beth Woodall and this is Cindy Lewis. We're from the Vineyard."

Beth is blonde and pretty. A young Louise, Elizabeth thinks. But Cindy has a limp and something is wrong with one arm. Elizabeth doesn't look at it directly.

"What can I do for you girls?"

"Oh, we just came to see you," Beth smiles brightly. "Paul and Louise thought we might cheer you up."

In the living room, Beth is the speaker. "We all knew your husband from the paper, Mrs. North. He was wonderful! My dad read every line he ever wrote, and says this town is lost without him." She pushes back her hair, anchors it behind one ear. Her nails, overlong, pale as seashells, seem to lag behind her fingers. "We've all been praying for you."

Elizabeth rubs a wet spot the hose has made on her skirt. "Thank you," she says, not looking up.

"I know how you feel," Beth says. "My boyfriend, Billy Moseley, was killed in a wreck last year. He'd been my boyfriend since grammar school, and we'd have gotten married someday, if he'd lived." Her eyes fill with tears. "We were just always . . . together."

Elizabeth remembers Billy. Handsome, polite. A star athlete killed by a drunk driver. She feels a quick stir of sympathy but, like everything painful since John died, it freezes before it can surface. Now it all seems packed in her chest, as in the top of a refrigerator so full the door will hardly shut. She looks back at Beth with dry, guilty eyes.

"Well, I'm all right now," Beth says. "But I thought it would kill me for a while. I didn't want to live without Billy, until I met the people at The Vineyard. They made me see it was God's will for him to die and me to live and serve the Lord. Now I know he's in heaven waiting for me, and it's not as bad as it was." She shrugs. "I try to help Billy's mother, but she won't turn it over to the Lord."

The room is growing dark. Elizabeth gets up to turn on more lights, which cast a roseate glow on their faces, delicate hands, slender feet in sandals.

"Would you girls like a Coke?" she asks.

Beth blinks to dry her eyes. "Yes, ma'am," she says. "Thank you. A Coke would be nice."

They follow Elizabeth to the kitchen, where she pours Coca-Cola into glasses filled with ice cubes.

"You must get lonesome here by yourself," Cindy says, looking around. "Are your children away from home or something?"

Elizabeth hands her a glass and paper napkin. "I don't have children, Cindy," she says. "My husband and I wanted a family, but couldn't have one. All we had was each other."

"Ah!" Beth says quickly. "We'll be your children, then. Won't we, Cindy?"

It is seven o'clock in the morning and Elizabeth is drinking instant coffee from an old, stained mug, staring dejectedly out the kitchen window. During the night, she'd had a dream about John. He'd been alive, not dead.

John had been editor-publisher of the *Wakefield SUN,* the town's weekly paper, had written most of the copy himself. In the dream, they'd been in bed for the night.

John had liked to work in bed, and she had liked to read beside him, so they'd gone to bed early as a rule. Propped up on pillows, he had worked on editorials, for which he'd been known throughout the state. At times, though, he had put aside his clipboard and taken off his glasses. When he turned her way, his eyes—blue-gray and rugged like the tweed jacket he'd worn so many winters—would take on a look that made the book fall from her hand. Later, sometimes, on to the floor.

In the dream, as he looked at her, the phone by their bed had rung. He'd forgotten a meeting, he said, throwing off covers. He had to get down there. It had already started, a meeting he couldn't afford to miss. Putting on his jacket, he'd stopped at the bedroom door.

"I'll be right back," he promised.

But he wasn't back and never would be, she'd been reminded, wide awake. In the dark, she'd checked the space beside her with her hand to be sure, and her loss had seemed new again, more cruel than ever, made worse by time. If only she could cry, she'd thought, like other widows. Cry, everyone told her. Let the grief out! But she couldn't. It was frozen and locked up inside her, a mass that wouldn't move.

She'd waked from the dream at two in the morning, and hasn't been back to sleep since. Now she's glad to be up with something to do, if it's only an appointment with her lawyer. She has sold John's business but kept the building, and the legalities are not yet over. She wants to be on time, is always on time. It's part of her fixation on detail, as if each thing attended to were somehow on a list that if ever completed would bring back meaning to her life.

In the fall she will go back to teaching school, but her heart is not in it as before. For twenty years she'd been, first of all, John's wife—from deadline to deadline, through praise, blame, long stretches of indifference. He couldn't have done it without her, he'd said, with each award and honor he'd been given.

Now no other role seems right for her, which is her problem, she's thinking, when the front door bell rings.

Louise is there in a fresh summer dress, her clean hair shining in the sun. She smells of something lightly floral.

"May I come in?"

Still in a rumpled nightgown and robe, aware of the telltale look in her eyes, Elizabeth opens the door wider, steps back. "I have an appointment," she says, and smiles as best she can. "But come in. There's time for a cup of coffee."

At the white table, Louise takes the place she'd had before. "I won't stay long," she says.

Elizabeth puts on a pot of coffee, gets out cups and saucers, takes a seat across from Louise. Outside, all is quiet. Stores and offices won't open until nine. So why is Louise in town at this hour?

"I was praying for you," she says, as if in answer. "But the Lord told me to come and see you instead."

Elizabeth stares at her. "God told you?"

Their eyes meet. Louise nods. "He wanted you to know that He loves you," she says. "He wanted to send you His love, by me." Her face turns a sudden bright pink that deepens and spreads.

Next door a car starts up and drives off. A dog barks. The coffee is ready and Elizabeth pours it. She's learned to drink hers black, but Louise adds milk and sugar.

"Come to The Vineyard with us next time, Elizabeth," Louise says suddenly. "Please."

This is what she came for, Elizabeth thinks, and it's more than an invitation. It's a plea, as from someone on the bank to a swimmer having trouble in the water.

"It could save your life!" Louise says.

The Vineyard is a narrow, shotgun-style house of the 1890s, last used as a dentist's office. It has one large front room, with two small rooms and a makeshift kitchen behind it. Having been welcomed and shown around, Elizabeth stands against the wall of the front room with Paul and Louise. The group is smaller than she'd expected, and not all Presbyterian. Some are from other churches as well, all smiling and excited.

Everything revolves around Steve, a young man in jeans who looks like a slight blonde Jesus. When Elizabeth is introduced, he looks her deep in the eyes.

"Elizabeth!" he says, as if he knows her already. "We were hoping you'd come. Welcome to The Vineyard."

He says no more and moves on, but she has felt his power like the heat from a stove. She finds herself following him around the room with her eyes, wishing she could hear what he says to other people.

The night is hot and windows are open, but no breeze comes through. Rotary fans monotonously sweep away heat, in vain. Someone brings in a pitcher of Kool-Aid, which is passed around in paper cups.

"Okay, people." Steve holds up his cup and raises his voice for attention. "Let's have a song."

Everyone takes a seat on the floor, in a ring shaped by the long narrow room. A masculine girl with short dark hair stands up. She tests one key then another, low in her throat, and leads off. "We are one in the Spirit, we are one in the Lord . . . "

Most of the singers are young, in shorts or jeans, but some are middle-aged or older. Of the latter, the majority are single women and widows like Elizabeth. The young people sit with folded legs, leaning comfortably forward, and the men draw up one leg or the other. But the women, in pastel pant suits and sleeveless dresses, sit up straight, like paper dolls bent in the middle.

The song gains momentum for the chorus, which ends, "Yes, they'll know-oh we are Christians by our love!"

"All right," Steve says. "Time to come to our Lord in prayer."

Someone clambers up to turn off the light switch and someone else lights a candle on the Kool-Aid table. In the dim light Steve reaches out to his neighbor on each side, and a chain of hands is quickly formed.

Without a hand to hold in her new single life, Elizabeth is glad to link in. She smiles at the young woman on her left and Paul on her right. Paul's hand no longer trembles but feels as it had in high school—not thrilling but dependable, a hand she could count on.

The room is suddenly hushed. "For the benefit of our visitor," Steve says, "we begin with sentence prayers around the circle, opening our hearts and minds to God."

Elizabeth feels a quick rush of misgiving. Oh, no! she thinks. I can't do this! She's never prayed out loud in her life except in unison, much less ad-libbed before a group.

But Steve has already started. "We thank you, Heavenly Father, for the privilege of being here. Guide us, we pray, in all we say and do, that it may be for the extension of your kingdom. We thank you again for each other, but above all for your blessed son Jesus, who is with us tonight, here in this circle."

On Steve's right, a young man with shoulder-length hair takes up at once. "I thank you, Lord, for turning me around. Until I found You, all I cared about was that bottle. But You had living water to satisfy my thirst. . . ."

Eagerly, one after the other, they testify, confess, ask help in bringing others to Jesus as Lord and Savior. They speak of the devil as if he's someone in town, someone they meet every day.

In her turn, a checkout girl from the supermarket starts to cry and can't stop. From around the circle come murmurs of "God bless you" and "We love you" until her weeping begins to subside.

"My heart's too full tonight," she chokes out, at last. "I have to pass."

On each side, Elizabeth's hands are gripped tighter. The back of her blouse is wet with sweat. The room begins to feel crowded and close.

"Praise God!" a man cries out in the middle of someone's prayer.

"Help me, Lord," a woman whimpers.

A teenage boy starts to pray, his words eerily unintelligible. Tongues?, Elizabeth wonders, electrified. They do it here, she's heard. But something nasal in his voice gives the clue, and she has a wild impulse to laugh. He's not speaking in tongues but is tongue-tied, from a cleft palate.

Too soon, she hears Paul's voice beside her, charged with emotion. He's praying about the sin of pride in his life, but she can't pay attention because she will be next. Heavy galloping hoofbeats seem to have taken the place of her heart.

When Paul is through, she says nothing. I pass flashes through her mind, but she doesn't say it. She is unable to decide on, much less utter, a word. Her hands are wet with cold perspiration. She tries to withdraw them, but Paul on one side and the young woman on the other hold on tight. Fans hum back and forth as her silence stretches out.

At last someone starts to pray out of turn, and the circle is mended. As the prayers move back toward Steve, she gives a sigh of relief and tries, without being obvious, to ease her position on the floor.

Steve gives a new directive. "We'll now lift up to God those with special needs tonight."

He allows them a moment to think, then leads off. "I lift up Ruth, in the medical center for diagnosis," he says. "Her tests begin in the morning."

They pray in silence for Ruth, for someone in the midst of divorce, for a man who's lost his job. An unnamed friend with an unidentified "problem" is lifted up.

Louise clears her throat for attention, then hesitates before speaking out. When she does, her voice is girlish and sweet as usual.

"I lift up Elizabeth," she says.

Elizabeth has avoided the telephone all day, though she's heard it ring many times. The weather is cloudy and cool, so she's spent the morning outside, weeding, hoeing, raking, and has come to one decision. She will not see the soul savers today.

Tomorrow, it may be, she can face them. Today, she will do anything not to. They were holding her up, she thinks, not for her sake but theirs. They refuse to look on the dark side of things, and they want her to blink it away too. If she can smile in the face of loss, grief, and death, so can they. They're like children in a fairy tale, singing songs, holding hands. Never mind the dark wood, the wolves and witches. Or birds that eat up the bread crumbs.

During lunch she takes the phone off the hook, eats in a hurry, and goes back out with magazines and a book. For supper she will go to Breck's for a barbecue and visit with whoever's there. When she comes back, the day will be over. "One day at a time," is the new widow's motto.

She is drying off from a shower when the front door bell rings. She doesn't hurry, even when it rings again and someone's finger stays on the buzzer. The third time, she closes the bathroom door, little by little, so as not to be heard. Gingerly, as if it might shock her, she flips off the light switch.

Soon there is knocking on the back door, repeated several times. She can hear voices but not words. When she continues to keep quiet, hardly breathing for fear they will somehow know or divine that she's there, the knocking stops and the voices, jarred by retreating footsteps, fade away. At last, through a sneaked-back window curtain, she sees the small red car moving off.

And suddenly, in her mind's eye, she can also see herself as from a distance, towel clutched like a fig leaf, hiding from a band of Christians out to save her soul!

For the first time in her widowhood, she laughs when she's alone. It happens before she knows it, like a hiccough or a sneeze. With re-found pleasure, she laughs again, more.

Still smiling, she dresses in a hurry and is about to walk out the back door when the front door bell rings.

This time she goes at once to face them. Beth and Cindy, plus Steve and two policemen, stare back at her. The policemen are in uniform, dark blue pants and lighter blue shirts, with badges, insignia, and guns on their belts. Obviously, they've been deciding how to get in the house without a key.

For a moment no one speaks. Then Beth, wide-eyed, bursts out, "You scared us to death, Mrs. North! We thought you had passed out or something. We knew you were in there because of your car."

"I didn't feel like seeing anyone today." Elizabeth's voice is calm and level. What has come over her?, she thinks. Where did it come from, that unruffled voice? She should be mad or upset, and she's not.

"Sorry we bothered you, Mrs. North," the older policeman says. "Your friends here were worried."

Out of the blue, Elizabeth is suffused all at once with what seems pure benevolence. For a split-second, and for no reason, she is sure that everything is overall right in the world, no matter what. And not just for her but for everyone, including the dead! The air seems rarified, the light incandescent.

"It was no bother," she says, half-dazed. "I thank you."

Steve has said nothing. His eyes are as calm as ever, the eyes of a true believer blessed or cursed with certainty. His focus has been steadily on her, but now it breaks away.

"Let's go, people," he says lightly. "We're glad you're okay, Elizabeth. God bless you."

Elizabeth has slept all night, for once. As she sits down to coffee and cereal, she is sure of one thing. She has to start what everyone tells her must be "a whole new life" without John, and she has to do it now. Though frozen and numb inside still, she can laugh. And she has experienced, beyond doubt, a mystical moment of grace.

When a car door slams out front, not once but twice, she gets up without waiting for anyone to ring or knock. It is Paul and Louise, for the first time not smiling. Paul has on khaki work clothes. Louise has brushed her hair on top, but underneath sleep tangles show.

In the living room, they sit leaning forward on the sofa. Paul rocks one knee nervously from side to side, making his whole body shake from the tension locked inside him.

"They should have come to us instead of going to the police," he says at once. "They just weren't thinking."

"No, it was my fault," Elizabeth says. "I should have gone to the door."

"Why didn't you?" Louise asks.

"Well . . . " She falls silent.

"Our meeting upset you?" Paul asks, in a moment.

Elizabeth's housecoat is old and too short. They catch her like this every time, she thinks. Why can't they call before they come, like everyone else? She begins to check snaps down her front.

"Level with us, honey," Paul says. "We're your friends. What upset you so much?"

Except for the faint click of a snap being snapped, the room is utterly quiet.

"We need to pray about this," Paul says. "Let's pray . . . "

"No!" Elizabeth is on her feet without thinking. "No, Paul. I can't!" She's out of breath as from running. "This has got to stop! I can't be in your Vineyard. You'll have to find somebody else!"

He's silent for so long a countdown seems to start. Then he stands up slowly, Louise beside him as if joined. At the door, with his hand on the knob, he turns.

"Well, Elizabeth," he says. "I guess it's time to say goodbye."

Her heart slows down as if brakes had been applied. The beats become heavy, far apart. She can feel them in her ears, close to her brain.

"I'm sorry, Paul!" she says quickly. Before his accusing eyes, she says it again, like holding out a gift she knows to be inadequate. "I'm sorry!"

But this time he has no joke or smile. Without a word, he takes Louise by the arm and guides her through the doorway.

Elizabeth watches them walk to the car, side by side but not touching. Paul opens the door for Louise, quickly shuts her in, and gets behind the wheel himself. The station wagon moves out of sight down the driveway.

Elizabeth's cereal is soggy, her coffee cold. She pushes it all away, props her elbows on the table, and buries her face in her hands. Suddenly, as from a thaw long overdue, she's crying. Sobs shake her shoulders. Tears seep through her fingers and run down her wrists. One drop falls on the glass top where, in morning sunlight, it sparkles like a jewel.

✒ No Sound in the Night

To Bunny the only thing new about Jean Goodwyn was her job. She was a local girl, and he'd known her back when she was in grade school and he was stuck in the sixth grade. He'd had to give up on school, but she sailed on through, college even. Now, less than six months after Bill Griffin dropped dead in his front yard, Jean was editor of the Chronicle.

Ed, the linotypist, and Henshaw, the ad man, shook their heads when they first heard it, but Jean won them over right away. She was nice, friendly, pretty, and all that. But the main thing was, she was good. They got the paper to bed on time every week now, and that made it easy on everyone.

She loved it too, you could tell. Every day when they got out the quads and gathered around the stone to shoot for Coca-Colas, her eyes sparkled. She was like a little girl let in on something big. She would shake the jessies as if her life depended on it, but seemed happiest of all when she lost and could pay for the setup.

She asked Ed and Henshaw all kinds of questions and listened so hard she forgot about her face. Sometimes her mouth would stay open so that it was comical to watch, but Bunny never felt like laughing.

"You can't learn that in school," she would say to Ed and Henshaw.

Bunny never expected her to notice him at all. He was only a printer's devil. Besides, he knew how he looked with his long front teeth, little watery eyes, and hands like paws. His nickname wasn't Bunny for nothing. But Jean treated him just like she did Ed and Henshaw.

"Where do you eat, Bunny?" she asked one day, as they were leaving the shop at noon. Ed and Henshaw were both married and went home to eat at noon.

"Luke's, most of the time," he said. He didn't go home because his mother, Mrs. Drake, sat with an old crippled lady in the daytime.

"Mind if I come with you?" Jean asked. "The Grille is awful."

As they walked down the street, everyone spoke and smiled. Bunny was proud, not embarrassed, to be walking with a girl for the first time in his entire thirty-two years. At Luke's they sat in a booth and ordered the regular dinner.

"This is good Southern cooking," Jean said, after a few bites. "Much better than the Grille. I'm glad you brought me here, Bunny."

"You know what they say?" Bunny heard himself asking. His upper lip was too short and had a way of working up and down, collecting spit, when he tried to talk. "They say 'When you eat at The Grille and read the Chronicle, you're still hungry and you don't know nothin.'"

Jean laughed so hard he laughed too.

"That's priceless, Bunny," she said.

"That was before you, though," he rushed to say. "They don't say that no more."

"Well, I'm glad." She studied a teaspoon encrusted with sugar stained brown, where someone had let it dip in his coffee. "Because I'm giving it all I've got."

"And . . . and . . ." Bunny was so excited his lip got in the way. If he just kept his mind on it, he could control it, his mother said. But he couldn't keep his mind on two things at once. "That's a lot!" he burst out.

He tried to think of something else to make Jean laugh but couldn't, and she wasn't the kind who talked when there was nothing to say. They ate their dinner and she drank a quick cup of coffee. Then Bunny could tell she wanted to get back to the shop.

"I enjoyed it, Bunny," she said, at the door to her office.

Her office was nothing but an oversized cubbyhole with a desk, telephone, two typewriters, and a couple of chairs. But she'd cleaned it up, found a table for the hot plate and percolator, and bought new mugs for everybody. Sometimes she brought yard flowers from home in a vase. On her desk she kept a framed picture of a young man Bunny didn't know.

That night when Bunny's mother, Mrs. Drake, asked what he had for dinner, he couldn't remember.

"Fish?" she said. "They had fresh catfish at the market today."

"No'm. We didn't eat fish."

"We?" Mrs. Drake's fork full of mashed potatoes stopped in midair.

"Me and Jean," he said.

"She ate with you?" Her eyes bored into his. "Did you pay for her dinner?"

"No'm." He stirred his iced tea. "She paid for her own."

Mrs. Drake spooned jelly from a jar that still had the label Pride of Alabama on it. Bunny thought she was going to talk about how hard it was to make ends meet, but she didn't.

After supper he dried the dishes while she washed. He carried out the garbage and locked the doors, front and back. After that, they sat in the living room until bedtime. He read comic books while she studied her Sunday School lesson and the Bible.

The Bible was where she found strength to bear all her crosses, she told people. Her crosses were labeled. A husband who deserted her, female trouble, the lack of money, and hardest to bear of all, a handicapped child.

Bunny would never forget the day she told him he was handicapped. He was in the first grade, and had brought home a report card with all D's and F's. She sat down, dried her hands on her apron, and told him. He kept his eyes on squares in the kitchen linoleum until she finished. His heart beat so hard he could hear it, but he didn't cry. The truth was, she didn't need to tell him. He already knew.

Tonight, in his narrow iron bed in the back room, he had a dream he'd dreamed over and over all of his life. He was trying to do something he couldn't do. This time he was taking an examination. First he couldn't read the questions, then he couldn't write the answers. He was trying so hard he thought he would burst with effort, when suddenly Jean Goodwyn was there. She picked up his paper, typed off the answers in rattling haste and handed back the paper with a smile. For the first time, he was saved before waking up.

The next morning he got up early, ate a bowl of corn flakes, and left before Mrs. Drake came in the kitchen. At the shop he'd already swept the whole place and emptied all the trash when Ed and Henshaw got there. He was dusting the office, just as he planned, when Jean came in.

"Hi, Bunny," she said, and put down the clipboard on which she collected notes and information about what was going on around town. "Did you know it's officially the first day of spring?"

He didn't know, but he should have. His heart was like a seed deep in the dirt, beginning to swell and push up. He took his dust rag and left right away. All he wanted was to see her.

They ate together most days after that. Around eleven he'd begin to watch the clock, and at twelve on the dot he'd mosey up toward her office. He never interrupted, but just stood around stacking leads and slugs in the type case or something until she looked up. If she happened to be out on a story, he waited at the front door, rain or shine, under the sign that said THE FAIRVIEW CHRONICLE. Once he stood there until ten minutes of one, then got a milk shake at the drug store, but he never told Jean. He let her think he went on to Luke's as usual.

Most of the time they talked about the paper and what was going on, but sometimes she told him things about herself. He knew she was an only child, and that her mother had died when she was fifteen. She lived at home with her father, who was in the lumber business and out of town a lot. She liked books and popular music, dancing and tennis, and was saving up money for a car. The one she had now, her Daddy's old car, was always breaking down at the wrong time. The name Bob Carter came up almost every day. It was his picture that she kept on her desk.

It wasn't long before Bob Carter dropped into the shop. He was movie-star handsome in a sports coat and tie, and he carried a tan briefcase. He came just before noon, when Bunny was about to go up toward the office.

Jean took him around to introduce him. Ed and Henshaw stopped what they were doing and went up to the stone, smiling and being pleasant. But Bob Carter didn't tarry long with them.

"And this is Bunny," she said, back at the casting box where he was. "Bunny's my pal."

"Is that right?" Bob said, not smiling.

Bunny hadn't washed his hands yet, and began wiping them on his pants, but Bob didn't offer to shake hands.

He kept looking around at the machinery as if he didn't want to get near it. The shop did look grey and grimy, Bunny knew, but it was a printing shop. They kept it the best they could.

Jean said they were on the way out for a quick barbecue. Did Bunny want to come?

But Bunny wasn't that dumb.

While she went for her coat, Bob Carter didn't go over to chat with Ed and Henshaw the way most people did. Instead, he went back up front and stood staring out at the street until she joined him.

When they left, Ed got up from the linotype machine and went up to the stone where Henshaw was setting ads.

"Well," he said. "What do you think?"

Henshaw kept the start of a smile on his face all the time, but sometimes, like now, his eyes weren't smiling. "He's a cold fish, idn't he?"

"Yeah." Ed wore a dark green eye shade that covered up all but his nose and mouth. He grinned. "Didn't even let us show him the type lice, did he?"

"What was he toting that briefcase for?" Henshaw asked. "Does he sell something?"

"Don't ask me." Ed shrugged. "Let's go home and eat."

Nobody waved at Bunny on the way to Luke's without Jean. Luke's glance slid over him as if he wasn't even there. Without Jean, he was only a dollar bill for the cash register. He read over the sign that said, "Knives, forks, and spoons are not medicine. Please don't take them after meals." He studied again the mounted fish on the wall, read over the titles of the juke box tunes, and went on back to work.

The next day Henshaw brought the lowdown on Bob Carter. He was from North Alabama, a hotshot insurance salesman for a company controlled by his father. Jean had met him at the University where he'd been a Big Man On Campus. According to Ed, he was stringing Jean along and had girls in other towns. Even though Jean was out, Ed lowered his voice when he told them. It was just between the three of them. That was understood.

"I'm not surprised," Ed said. "Pretty boys like that get spoiled. They don't want to settle down."

"I feel sorry for her, though," Ed said. "I think she's got it bad."

Bunny said nothing, although they included him. "My boy has some true friends," Mrs. Drake always said when someone mentioned Ed or Henshaw. "Bunny may not be as bright as some, but those men at the printing office think the world and all of my boy."

It wasn't long before Jean came in one morning with a ring on her left hand. So Henshaw must have been mistaken, after all. Jean didn't mention the ring but they all noticed. They couldn't help it, Ed said. It was a rock.

Bunny tried not to believe it. He'd learned long ago not to look into the future. The present was better that way. And since Jean never mentioned getting married or leaving, he ignored the possibility. Besides, things kept happening. Like the time Bob dropped in to find her out on a story.

"When do you expect her?" he wanted to know.

What could they say? She was covering an all-day farm affair and could be gone for hours. They told him they thought she'd be back pretty soon, if only to check in and out. It depended on what was going on out there.

He'd left right away.

"But what did he say?" Jean wanted to know when she got back in half an hour. "Is he coming back later?"

What he'd said, though they didn't tell her, was, "Maybe I should have an appointment." And he didn't come back at all that day.

But the main thing that kept Bunny's hope alive was a simple fact. No matter who else Jean loved, she still loved the Chronicle.

"You've got a real editor down there now, Bunny," people would say when he went out to deliver printing jobs. "You fellows better hang on to that girl."

In his awkward, loping gait he would hurry all the way back to the shop to tell Jean. Except for a little society news that a lady wrote at home, sports news that Henshaw took care of, and a few obituaries that Ed could do, Jean wrote the whole paper. She had a key to the shop and usually went back until nine or ten o'clock at night. That was when she wrote editorials. Bill Griffin had used clips from other papers most of the time, but Jean took pride in writing her own.

The first time a big daily picked one up, Henshaw was the one who found it. Henshaw was a sports fan and looked through the papers first thing each morning. He had the Post-Herald all spread out on the stone when he gave a sudden whoop.

"Hey, ho!" he called out. "How about this!"

"Your team win?" Ed called from the back.

"Come look," he said. "Everybody!"

With a stained finger (their hands were always stained with printer's ink) he was pointing to the column headed "State Editors

Are Saying." There, along with the rest, was an editorial titled "Keep Your County Clean," and beneath it in eight-point Italic type, the Fairview Chronicle.

"Now that's all right!" Ed said, standing, looking.

Bunny's lip was working madly. "Ain't it?" he said. He couldn't stand still. "Ain't it, though!"

Jean's eyes filled up with tears. Without a word, she turned and went back to her office.

Henshaw cut out the whole page and thumbtacked it to her office door. After that the News and the Advertiser picked up Jean's editorials often. After about eight, Henshaw stopped tacking them to the door.

One Wednesday morning in May, press day, Jean came in with a large magnolia blossom. "First of the season," she said, holding it up. "Maybe I can eke out a paragraph or two about that. There's just not any news."

But just as Henshaw was about to lock up the forms early, the phone rang. In a minute Jean came to the office door with a changed face.

"There's been a murder," she said. "A waitress out where we go for barbecue shot a man named Shine."

"Shine?" Ed said, frowning beneath his eye shade. "There's not but one Shine. I know him."

"And I know the waitress," Jean said, reaching for copy paper and a pencil. "I'm on my way, you all."

The phone began to ring and keep ringing. Violence was big news in Fairview, and everyone wanted to tip off the paper. Also, everybody knew everybody else and the interest was personal.

Jean didn't get back until they were ready to go to lunch. When she did, they all gathered around for the straight of it. Her face looked naked. Her eyes were glassy.

"I talked to the girl," she said, looking at them as if they were off at a distance instead of right there. "She was down in the jail, locked up behind bars.

"She says she did it. No question of that. She'd been living with Shine for two years, nursing him over drunks, paying his bills. She said she's loved him since she was fifteen years old, couldn't help herself, and he kept telling her he'd marry her as soon as he got on his feet.

"But he went off to Montgomery, met a young girl, and married her all in the same week. The waitress didn't even know it until he came back to get his clothes. She says she doesn't know what came over her. She just opened the drawer, took out the pistol, and pulled the trigger. She says she doesn't care what they do to her. She doesn't want to live any more, anyway."

No one spoke. Bunny kept hitching up his pants.

"That's what love can do to you," Jean said. When she picked up her notes, the ring on her left hand sparkled. "I'll go try to write it."

"There's coffee in the pot," Ed said. "And the AP man called. Wants you to give him the facts."

"I'll call him," she said.

She went into her office and closed the door. They hurried to lunch and back. In her office the typewriter rattled, fell silent, rattled again. People drifted in and out to talk about the murder. Shine got what was coming to him, everyone agreed.

But what would become of the waitress? She ought to get a medal, a secretary from down the street said.

"She can plead temporary insanity," Ed said.

"And she'll plead right," Henshaw said. "That's what love is, temporary insanity."

Everyone laughed except Bunny. He didn't want them to bad-mouth love.

The afternoon began to wane. The town clock struck and struck again. Young boys, their shirttails out and pants stained green, began drifting home from baseball.

Finally Jean came out and handed Ed a few pages.

"This is just the facts," she said. "But I'm trying to write that interview down in the jail. It'll take a while longer. Can you stand it?"

Another wait would mean midnight or later, but no one minded. News was their business. If Jean could get it, they could damn well print it, Henshaw said.

Ed shook a cigarette out onto the stone. "Let's go home and come back," he said. "That way she won't feel like we're waiting so hard."

Bunny went in to see if there was anything she wanted before he left. Before she could answer, Bob Carter was standing at the door behind him. This time he had an appointment, it seemed.

"Oh, Bob," Jean said. Her face lit up, then the light wavered. "I tried to call you, but you'd already left. Did you hear about the murder?"

"About ten times," he said. "So come on. Let's go get something to eat."

"But I can't leave." Jean pointed helplessly to the pages scattered over her desk. "I have to finish so we can go to press. They're waiting on me! Could you go to the picture show or something until I'm through?"

Bunny eased out and Bob shut the door to the office. Water was running noisily in the back, so Ed would be washing his hands. Henshaw was slowly and carefully rolling down his sleeves.

"Bobby-boy might change our plans," he said.

They waited to see. Jean's voice could be heard explaining and explaining. The door finally opened and Bob came out alone. Without looking their way, he walked straight to the front door and out. When Jean didn't follow, the three of them left together, as quietly as they could.

All during supper, Mrs. Drake fussed at Bunny for getting so excited over things. The murder had nothing to do with him, thank the Lord, so why didn't he calm down and eat his supper? Someday he'd learn to control himself, she hoped. What did he want to go running back down there for, anyway?

"I have to run the cylinder press, Mama," he said, which was true, but only in part. He wanted to go by Luke's and take Jean a sandwich. Toasted bacon, lettuce, and tomato was what she liked.

Luke's was crowded because the high school crowd was there, so Bunny had to sit on a counter stool and wait. It would take two forevers tonight, he was thinking, when suddenly he jumped as if someone had touched him on the shoulder.

Not three feet away, Bob Carter stood in front of the cash register, ready to pay his check. To Bunny's relief, Bob hadn't seen or recognized him, so he pivoted his stool in the opposite direction and kept his head down.

Bob asked permission to use the phone long distance, then came behind the counter to place the call. The phone was almost at Bunny's elbow, so he couldn't help hearing what was said.

"Long time no see," Bob said, to someone at the other end of the line. He listened for a minute, then said, "Well, I really want to see you and talk to you. What are you doing tonight around eight?"

Bunny didn't use bad words. They were for grown men not boys. In spite of his age he knew he was less man than boy. "Like a child," he'd heard people say when they talked about him. But hurrying back to the shop with Jean's sandwich and milk shake, he kept saying over and over, son of a bitch, that son of a bitch. He didn't know he was saying it out loud until he heard his own voice. "Talking to yourself again," his mother would say.

Jean's typewriter was going. When she looked up, it took a minute to change the focus of her attention.

"Why, Bunny," she said. "What a nice thing to do! I was hungry and didn't know it."

He waited until she opened it all up, then turned to go.

"Don't go," she said. "Did you see Bob's car anywhere around?"

Bunny hitched up his pants. "No," he said. "I didn't see it."

"I thought he might wait," she said.

With Bunny, amenities weren't necessary. Like a pet, he could be present without having to be noticed, so he sat looking at the floor while Jean ate in silence. From outside, young, high-pitched laughter could be heard from time to time. Footsteps and voices went by. With the last bite, Jean wadded up the wrapping paper and paper napkin, stuffed them into the empty milk carton.

"Thanks, Bunny," she said and, without warning, put her head down on her typewriter and began to sob.

Bunny had no idea what to do or say. Stumbling out, he was glad no one was there to see his burning face. Something elemental, which he felt to be shameful, had stirred within him.

They went to press at nine o'clock and finished up at midnight. Jean stayed to the end, then Henshaw took them all home in his car. Riding down the deserted streets with the town asleep around them, they were somehow proud of the lateness of the hour and their own exhaustion. They were newspaper people, trustees of the news, obscure members of a great and honorable fraternity.

The next morning was a red-letter Morning After. Unable to turn their attention from the night just past, they were like people walking down the street looking backward. Jean was late for the first time, and since there was nothing to do that couldn't wait, Ed, Henshaw, and Bunny stood around the stone talking to people who came in from the street.

"That interview with the waitress was something," one of the barbers dropped in to say. "That was one hell of a story. Almost had me crying."

"Almost had me crying when I set it," Ed said.

The whole town seemed to agree, and people kept dropping in all day to compliment Jean and the Chronicle.

"It took a murder and Jean Goodwyn to put Fairview on the map," someone said. The story, with local names and quotes, was in all the daily papers.

"Yes, if I did steal a pig, I want my name in the paper!" someone quipped.

Ed, Henshaw, and Bunny were like members of a winning team, while Jean was carried around on the shoulders of the town. But in the midst of victory, she seemed cast down. She smiled, but her smiles were on the surface. Her thank-yous were sad. For the rest of the week she seemed in a daze, and on Monday morning she wasn't wearing the ring. It was conspicuous by its absence, Henshaw said. He and Ed were relieved.

"She'll get over it," Henshaw said. "And thank her lucky stars someday."

But the day of thanksgiving was a long time coming and Jean seemed sadder than ever. At lunch she said little and ate less. She became thin and lost her car keys, misplaced her clip board. She drank coffee and sent Bunny to the drug store for aspirin. Bunny's heart ached to look at her and, longing to comfort her, he recognized at last the yearning that had plagued him for weeks. He wanted to touch her.

The idea itself made him tremble. At the thought, his hands would shake so that he had to hide them. His voice, when he spoke, was more tremulous than ever. His upper lip was in constant motion.

"What on earth is wrong with you, Bunny?" Mrs. Drake wanted to know, with rising irritation.

Jean seemed not to notice. She covered the news as conscientiously as ever, but came up with no human interest features or editorial gems. For the first time she used a few clips.

"When a lady's in love she loves everything," Henshaw said. "When its over, nothing looks good for a while."

He and Henshaw tried to jolly things up, but there were few jokes and not much laughter. They were helpless before what Henshaw called Jean's broke heart.

Bunny became more and more possessed. He had no words for what he felt. He only knew it was with him day and night. In his bed in the back room, he slept and waked, imagining himself holding Jean's hand, putting his arm around her. Beyond that even his daydreams wouldn't go, for a long-buried memory rose up to stop them.

Years ago in childhood, he'd liked a little girl. He sat behind her in school, hung around her at recess, gave her pencils and candy. She had tolerated him kindly, until one day in a deserted hall he tried to kiss her. The instant she recognized what he meant to do, her eyes flew wide in horror. Shrinking back, her mouth made a small, round zero of revulsion. She would have screamed, he knew, if he hadn't backed off and run away. The next day she changed her seat, and never spoke to him again.

Mrs. Drake was threatening to take him to Dr. Long, to see what was wrong with him, when the news came that Bob Carter had married. His bride was the daughter of a Wiregrass cattleman, rich as Croesus, someone said. Her picture, carried in several papers, was not in a wedding dress. The marriage had been an elopement, they heard.

"Well," Ed said, looking at the three-column spread in the bride's hometown paper. "This will kill or cure Jean."

At first, it did seem more than she could stand. The day she found out, she stayed shut up in her office most of the time. At lunch she ordered soup and black coffee.

"You better eat," Bunny said. "You'll be so skinny you won't even cast no shadow."

"Don't worry, Bunny," she said, and her voice was suddenly braced with something new. "I'll feel better soon. Tonight I'm going to start a series of stories on a hospital. That's something the whole county needs, and could have."

Tonight! Bunny thought, as if a timer had gone off in his brain. Tonight she would be at the office alone.

He hardly knew what he did for the rest of the day. Long ago, in secret, beneath and beyond his will or sanction, he had somehow accepted the fact that he would tell her he loved her. Now with an opportunity, it was all he could do to keep up a normal front. He had already melted lead and cast plates, but forgot all about the printing jobs he was supposed to deliver.

"What's the matter with you, boy?" Henshaw asked, when the failure came to light. "You better get on the ball."

It was one of the few reprimands he'd ever needed. He'd had hundreds of corrections, patient and impatient, explanations kind and exasperated. But he was always excused and forgiven. "Bunny does the very best he can," he'd overheard Ed and Henshaw tell people many times.

After making the deliveries, he was late getting home, only to face Mrs. Drake, a living obstacle in housedress and apron.

Why don't you have time to eat supper, what have you got to do at the shop, what do you want to take a bath now for?, she wanted to know.

He would have liked to put on his best pair of pants but knew he'd never get away with that, so he dressed in clean work clothes and hoped Mrs. Drake would cut short her lecture on dirtying up so much for her to wash. Combing his hair with scented oil, he gave extra attention to the cowlick on top, but never really looked at his face in the mirror. Not once did he meet the eyes fringed with pale, rabbity lashes. Trembling inside and out, he turned off the old fashioned light bulb that hung from the ceiling and hurried from his room.

Mrs. Drake didn't mention the clothes, though she noticed, he knew. She sat with her Bible and looked at him through gold-rimmed bifocals. She looked tired and worried and, for once, said nothing.

He almost ran from the room and from her eyes, but out of the house, the darkness reassured him. In the night, he might have been any other fellow on his way to see a girl.

He hurried until he came to the main street with its lights and people. A service station was open on the downtown corner, and a man he knew sat tilted back in a chair outside the door.

"Evenin', Bunny," the man said as usual.

"Evenin'," Bunny said, and hurried on.

When he came to the Power Company he slowed down, though his heart was beating faster than ever. Near the hardware store, he began to shiver as if winter had set in. He passed the furniture store and then, to put things off, stopped to look in the jewelry store window. A display of wedding rings was centered with a doll dressed up as a June bride. He jerked away as if a blinding light had been flashed in his eyes.

At the picture show, rows of yellow lights seemed to expose him inside and out, and he would have rushed by except the Chronicle was only two doors down. So he forced himself to stop and read over every movie title for the month of July. The girl in the ticket window watched him with an expression he'd seen on faces all of his life.

"How you doin', Bunny?" she asked kindly.

"Fine," he said, as always.

In front of the Chronicle, he stopped. The palms of his hands were wet with sweat. His heart was beating up in his throat.

The light was on in Jean's office, but the shade was down. She would be at her typewriter, a crook-necked lamp aimed at the page on which she worked. When he went in, she'd look up and smile. And then?

Why wouldn't he face it? The minute she read his mind, her mouth would open and make a small round zero of disbelief. From then on, everything would be ruined.

The truth sank in like a weight, pushing his heart back in place and slowing his pounding pulses. As if caught at something shameful, he turned to see if anyone was watching. No one was, so he started back down the street, looking both ways like a runaway colt.

In Fairview they roll up the sidewalks at eight o'clock, people said. So no one had seen him except the girl at the ticket window. But then a car went by, and another. They might wonder what he was doing down here by himself at this hour, so he turned the corner to the post office. It was perfectly natural for him to go there. He went at least twice, every day of his life.

But he didn't go inside the building. Instead, he stood outside and filled his lungs, then exhaled as if breathing out more than air. Up and down the street, everything was closed.

But back on the main street, one of the drug stores was still open. Like a lost shadow, he moved in that direction.

Not many people were in the store, and the ones who were there looked tired and sleepy. So no one seemed to notice as he went behind the rows of over-the-counter drugs, toiletries, and gift-boxed candy. From the lowest shelf of the magazine rack, he picked out five comic books, two western, two horror, and one cartoon.

"What's the good word, Bunny?" the cashier asked, when she took his money.

"I don't know it," he said, without meeting her eyes.

Outside, he put the sack of comic books under one arm and turned toward home. A gentle breeze lifted a tuft of carefully combed hair and dropped it down on his forehead, where it seemed to belong. He walked fast to put the heart of town behind him, then moved more slowly down the street toward the little house they'd rented for so many years. His footsteps on the sidewalk made no sound in the night.

The Birthday Cake

Two, two, two, she kept saying on her way to the phone, so she wouldn't forget how many cupfuls she'd put in the bowl. Her memory, like an old servant no longer efficient, was not to be trusted, and she was making hot rolls for Charles. Feeling young, and happy.

"Fern?" Her sister, Maude Ellen, was out of breath. "Have you heard about Sadie? She's dead! That girl found her when she went to work this morning . . ." She stopped short. "What's that girl's name?"

Fern thought at once of her dining room table, leaves removed, already set for two. Cutwork place mats, champagne flutes, a centerpiece of jonquils picked with dew still in their cups. Charles, who was Dr. Albright from North Alabama, was to be here by suppertime. It was his birthday, his sixty-ninth, and he was going to propose to her tonight, she was certain.

"Well, are you there?" Maude Ellen asked sharply. "What's wrong with you today?"

"I'm in the midst of something, Maude. Somebody's coming to supper here tonight."

"Oh, you'll have to put that off."

"I can't put it off. It's his birthday."

There was a pause. "His birthday?"

"Yes, I was going to tell you. Someone I met on that tour."

"I see." Maude Ellen had been urging her to find someone for years. Now the line buzzed with silence. "Well, I'm sorry," she said, with a sigh. "It always comes at the worst possible time."

Fern felt like sitting down but went on standing up, gripping the hard receiver. Charles was to be on the road in an hour. His suit bag would be ready to go in the car. So how could she tell him not to come? On the other hand, she couldn't let him come for the funeral of a stranger, someone he'd never heard of before.

"I'll go on over there, then," Maude Ellen said at last. "Maybe you can think of something. I won't even say I told you."

At the sink, Fern stared out the window. Sadie, of all people! Like the Rock of Gibraltar. Two days ago she'd been out and about, in the grocery store buying bananas. Now she was gone forever.

Fern took a deep breath and released it. She was still here, thank God. She'd be perfectly happy to stay on forever if she didn't see, every day, what was happening to Maude Ellen, ten years her senior.

And not just Maude. Most of her friends were as bad or worse, falling apart in general. Holding on to the stair rails, dialing wrong numbers, driving so slow in cars people would risk anything, even head-on collision, to get around them. In fact, old people were getting to be a problem all over. For every one who died, several more lived on, to be eighty, ninety, sometimes a hundred. She brushed off her apron and rinsed her hands.

On the counter, on a tall glass cake stand, a finished layer cake was ready for the candles. The cake, chocolate with white icing, was from a recipe called "Dark Decadence," sinfully rich but delicious. She'd never had a cake turn out better, she thought. From mixing to frosting, everything had gone right, even the tricky seven-minute icing.

In fact, until now, everything had gone right since the day she met Charles Albright. She'd noticed him at once that day on the bus, and had waited for his wife to appear. The ones still attractive always had wives, whether present at the moment or not. But when they stopped for lunch in Meridian and he took the seat next to hers, he'd let her know right away that his wife wasn't living, that he'd lost her from a stroke two years ago. Now he just rattled around the house by himself, he said, smiling bravely.

So they'd had three lovely days in Natchez, plus the rest of the one going over and another coming back, when she hadn't even wanted to go on that trip. She'd only gone because one of her best friends was director of the tour and someone had dropped out at the last. Also, because it was spring and she'd been . . . well, lonely.

When Charles had asked to come down so soon, all the way from Decatur, he said it was to talk about their future, face to face, not on the phone. At their age, he said, they couldn't afford to put things off and he'd known from the start he was hooked.

She wanted him to come, could hardly wait to see him. If only she could avoid that decision! She'd worked too hard for the peace she enjoyed to risk it on anything chancy, and marriage was the chanciest thing on earth, she'd found out.

Sadie was Sarah Ainsworth, someone she'd known all her life, lived next door to as a child, someone almost like family. Sadie's children all called her "Aunt Fern," and she should be over there now, answering the phone, doing something.

Through the window, she looked out to what seemed an idyllic spring. Her redbud was in full fuchsia bloom. Beside it, an ornamental peach was white with blossoms. The grass, bright green, was sprinkled with petals from a pear tree she'd planted as a bride. The handle of the spade had made a blister in her hand. When she showed it to Robert, her young husband, he had kissed it.

"You did that for me!" he'd said, drawing her close in the chilly afternoon, while a huge red sun went down behind them. They'd gone inside arm in arm, and she'd thought that kind of happiness could go on forever.

Pears had been Robert's favorite fruit. But by the time the tree began to bear, she'd found the note from his lover.

He'd promised to break it off after that, but hadn't for as long as he lived. His girlfriend was a waitress at the Korner Kafe, where he'd had breakfast at six every morning except weekends. A hard-working dentist, he'd also gone back to the office at night every week. To do lab work, he'd said.

Think of an excuse, Maude Ellen had said, about going to Sadie's. Pretend nobody told you. But Maude knew full well that she wouldn't, or couldn't. At the thought, familiar forces—conscience, sense of duty, old loyalties—began to mass inside her like antibodies.

By the phone in her den, she put on her glasses. Charles' number was still penciled-in beside those of her children (in Georgia, Tennessee, North Carolina), and police, ambulance, family doctor. She didn't yet know where his number should go, or if it would even stay. But she'd often thought lately, all else aside, how nice it would be to have a doctor in the house. Retired would be perfect, always on call. She read his number twice, then sat down and dialed.

"Charles?" Her voice trembled as she spilled out the news.

He was silent at first, then sighed, "Well, my dear," he said. "These things happen. I'll come when it's over, when you're free. Don't worry about this another minute. I'm just sorry you've lost an old friend."

Before they hung up, he said, "There's something you can do for me, though, if you will. I know the ritual, and all you have to do. So take my cake to your friend's house with you, so you won't have to cook. To save you that much would please me."

As she drove up, Sadie's son, John, from Jackson, Mississippi, was turning into the driveway. Beside him on the front seat was his wife, and in the back someone with a head of outlandish blonde hair. That would be their daughter, the one at Ole Miss, who was giving them all such a fit. The one who, in spite of everything, had been Sadie's heart.

Fern parked down the street beyond Maude Ellen's old Dodge, under an oak tree not yet leafed out. Maude Ellen would have been one of the first to arrive. A nurse for forty years before retiring, she considered it up to her, at times like this, to keep everyone from going to pieces. She could almost be back in uniform, a little white cap on her head.

In the living room women stood around like a household staff, waiting for the doorbell to ring. Sadie's two daughters had come, they said, but were still in the back making plans with the preacher.

Maude Ellen had gone on to the kitchen, where someone had brought in a coffee urn, big enough for a crowd, but without any instructions. Maude Ellen had evidently put herself in charge, inspecting each part, thinking out loud, while two young women, eager to take over, looked on.

"I'll go on to the dining room," Fern said, to their backs.

Sadie had lived alone, and her house was a mess. The girl did the cleaning and the living room was straight, but the rest would have to be tidied. Sadie couldn't throw things away and, besides all that, wanted everything anyone had given her out to be seen, tacky and fine together. A papier-mâché egg Fern had brought last Easter was still on top of the television set.

"Fern Wilson brought me that," she would have said, if anyone noticed. "There's candy in it. Have a piece."

What would Sadie think of this business with Charles? Fern wondered. Everyone in Wakefield knew about the girlfriend. Though she'd never talked about it, she could tell by their eyes that they knew. Even her children had felt the looks, sympathetic and pitying, but also deadly curious.

"What's wrong with us, Mama?" they'd asked, one by one.

She'd given them hugs, hot chocolate with marshmallows, and her full, undivided attention, but had let the truth come out on its own, like Santa Claus and the Tooth Fairy. Without meaning to be false, she'd kept up a united front. The truth was, Robert was a good man, at home as much as most men. He'd been good to the children and good to her. Besides that, she loved him. She'd stood up in church, a virgin in a white veil of illusion, and made vows, brought his children into the world. How could she take it all back?

After the note, to keep her sanity, she'd begun confiding in Maude Ellen, who already knew from the gossip.

"Leave him!" Maude Ellen had said, more than once. "Take those children and let him go to the devil!"

"Leaving wouldn't fix it," she'd said.

Cards and letters, snapshots and clippings, were scattered over Sadie's dining room table. Fern put them all in an empty cardboard box discarded on the floor near a tea cart. Afterwards she dusted, and spread a cloth on the table. When someone came in with an arrangement of flowers, the table was ready for a centerpiece.

She moved on to the den, not yet in use, but was stopped at the door by what she saw.

Across the room, Johnny—fifty years old and over six feet tall—leaned against the wall with his arms above his head. An only son, he'd been accused by his sisters of being their mother's favorite all his life. His hands, flat against the wall, might have been nailed through flesh and bone.

Fern retreated at once to the kitchen, where things had changed by now. A friendly aroma of coffee filled the air. Cartons of soft drinks, stacks of paper plates, packages of potato chips had arrived. Counters had been cleared off for the influx of food now being prepared in kitchens all over Wakefield.

Everyone moved and spoke with purpose, eager to do for Sadie what she had done for them, in times of joy and sorrow, so willingly while she lived.

At the funeral home that night, Sadie's children and grandchildren, in Sunday clothes, received callers. The daughters' faces looked raw, as from a day at the beach, makeup having been thrown away in wads of damp Kleenex. Johnny's smiles seemed called up out of necessity, to prevent the collapse of his face.

"What will we do without her?" people kept repeating like a litany.

Grandchildren, looking limp and uncertain, stood around in a cluster. Their shoulders dropped. Their arms seemed overlong.

Having spent weeks with their grandmother each summer, they no doubt thought she would be there forever. Their eyes were wide but evasive, as if they'd been brought in to something for adults, not them.

Where was the one with the hair? Fern wondered. Nowhere to be seen here tonight.

Ah, Sadie! Some things it's best not to know, all in all—like the contents of that note long ago. The note hadn't been dashed off in haste on the order pad of a waitress. It had been composed, then copied with care, like a classroom assignment to be graded. "Dear Dr. Wilson," it began.

Fern never forgot one sentence, word for word. "Before I knew you," the sentence said, "my life was nothing."

At the end of the room, the casket was backed with a high wall of flowers, though the family had requested donations to charities instead. Only death could make Sadie lie down in a room full of people, Fern thought. She should be up, limping around, trying to cheer everyone up. Her hands had grown dry and bone-hard, grasping like claws whoever happened to stop in front of her. As her eyesight failed, she'd brought her face up close to everyone else's, her breath like gusts of recycled air.

The casket was open so that anyone who cared to could look. Fern preferred to remember Sadie as she'd been when alive, but Maude Ellen reported that she looked nice, in a silk dress the color of her eyes.

Fern leaned close to Maude Ellen and whispered, deadpan, "Her eyes weren't open, were they?"

A smile flickered across Maude Ellen's face. "Sometimes you make me ashamed to even know you!" she said. Her lips barely moved, like the lips of a ventriloquist.

For the first time today, Fern looked closely at her sister. Maude Ellen's skin was gray. Magnified by thick lenses, her eyes were like those of a dog they'd once had, who lived to be fourteen years old. Sad, tired, defenseless against what lay ahead.

Fern took her gently by the arm. "Let's go home, Maudie," she said. "It's late."

They were in church the next day a half-hour early. "If we're not there ahead of time, we won't get a seat," Maude Ellen had said, over and over. "Everybody in town will be there."

In the fast-filling pews, people stared straight ahead, toward the pulpit, the choir, the stained-glass windows. Fern moved close to Maude Ellen to make extra room, then shut it all out with a question. What would she say to Charles when he asked her?

"I want to Charles, but . . ."

She could imagine the surprise on his face. "What do you mean, but?"

She would tell him then about the girlfriend, the shock and humiliation. The strain all those years of trying to keep going at home, then hold up her head and smile on the street. She would confess how she'd tortured herself with a question she still couldn't answer. Why would Robert need or want someone else, if she hadn't failed as a wife?

Of course she didn't think the same thing would happen with Charles, at his age. But all kinds of heartache were possible, even to be expected, the moment you gave yourself to another.

"Don't ask me!" she could almost hear herself tell Charles, rather than risk it.

The organist, with a strong, sure touch, was playing hymn after hymn. "The Old Rugged Cross," "Abide with Me," "Just As I Am," "Shall We Gather at the River?"

Fern began to feel a rising swell in her chest. To subdue it, she began to count floral offerings down front. How much had it all cost? she wondered. An extravaganza of flowers, on stands and in sprays, with potted plants below, covered the entire front of the church. There was a cross of white carnations, the red outline of a heart on a stand, circles of white for eternity. In the mass of color and design, she soon lost count, lost interest. She couldn't multiply such figures in her head.

Sadie's casket, covered with pink roses, was wheeled in and positioned. Everyone stood, openly staring as the family, brought low by loss, filed humbly in.

The young minister read at length from scripture and psalms, then made a ringing statement. "I thank God today for the life of Sarah Ainsworth. Our 'Miss Sadie.'"

"I will never forget the first time I went to call on her when I came here, a new young preacher in a strange town. I wasn't with her long before I knew I had one friend here already, and I still remember how good that made me feel. We had a cup of coffee, a piece of her famous pound cake, a fine visit."

"When it was time for me to go, she said, 'Now I want to tell you something, something to remember. This is a good place to be, as good as any, but don't expect it to be easy. Don't even want it to be easy, because then you wouldn't grow!'" He paused, as if to brace himself. "And then she said, 'I will be praying for you. Every night, on my knees.'"

Fern found herself fighting back an impulse to sob out loud, like the primitive mourners sometimes shown on TV. Sadie would have said that, she thought, and would have done it. All her life she'd been religious, never wanting to be safely wild as she, Fern had. And even Maude, who would try anything once when they were young.

Sadie and Maude had married longtime beaux, the only boys who asked them, and both of their marriages had turned out fine. She, though, had a choice, and had settled without a qualm on Robert, the quiet one.

Now and then over the years she'd run into his girlfriend on the street or in a store. When it happened, both their faces had blanched so that it seemed for a moment they might faint in a heap, together. The girlfriend had not been someone she could hate. Without background or opportunity, she was a true and natural beauty, clearly no seductress. Because of Robert she never married, but lived and died alone, pathetically soon after he did. Her name was Irene.

The affair had made no one happy, least of all Robert. Holding Fern once, he had broken into sobs. "I want you to know . . ." he tried to explain, but only sobbed so loud she'd been afraid the children, still at home, would wake up and hear.

"Sssh!" she'd whispered. "Sssh. It's all right!"

Separation and divorce had not been mentioned.

It was understood that Maude Ellen would drive her own car to the cemetery. Years ago she'd announced that she didn't like to ride with other people. With Fern, never.

"Just look at those cars!" she said now, watching them pull out and line up blocks ahead, behind a police car. "I don't feel like getting jammed in there today. Do you? Let's just wait. Let them all go!"

So they were among the last to reach the grave site, on the far side of the cemetery, the old, hilly part. Ainsworth markers, going back a hundred and fifty years, shared with those of other early settlers the gentle slopes and hollows. Around it all, a line of trees curved as in fraternal embrace. But the trees looked somehow wintry, the cedars and pines as dark as ever, the big trees still mostly bare. Only a mist of yellow-green leaves along the branches, a few dogwoods in bloom, confirmed the fact of spring.

On the edge of the crowd, heels sunk deep in leaf-covered loam, Fern could neither see nor hear—except for brief glimpses of the preacher's head, the rise and fall of his voice—what went on under the green funeral tent. When people bowed their heads, she bowed hers. When they said the Lord's prayer, she joined in. Otherwise, she could only imagine the rose-covered casket not yet lowered, the family seated on folding straight chairs, their feet precisely side by side on artificial grass. With downcast eyes, they would be holding themselves together like clenched fists, for just a little longer.

She would have liked to see the bad girl's face but couldn't, thanks to Maude.

A March-like wind had sprung up, and people huddled against it. Shoulder to shoulder with the rest, she felt at once rooted to the spot and part of a slow-moving throng, of those gone before and those still to come. On her right, Maude Ellen stood up straight in her crepe-soled shoes, defying the wind in an old winter suit. But her arm, touching Fern's, was trembling.

Fern, too, felt a chill, the chill of standing by someone's grave, glad it wasn't her own. It was a lonely feeling, even with Maude Ellen beside her. Sisters went only so far, she supposed. It was Charles that she wanted and needed. She thought of his eyes that had seen so much (and still no glasses!), his fine physician's hands. With his silver hair, he looked what he was, a Southern gentleman.

But why was this taking so long? she thought, trying to spot a wristwatch near by. Almost at once there was a hush. Even the wind grew still. Words became distinct, as if etched on the stilled air. "Earth to earth, ashes to ashes, dust to dust . . ." The preacher said a final Amen and began to shake hands with the family.

The crowd broke apart all at once. Among the departing faces were those Fern didn't know, as well as some she hadn't seen for months or years. Young people she'd known in the past looked like the fathers or mothers of themselves. Of the ones her own age, nearly everyone's hair was gray, or darker, lighter, more golden than ever.

A strange young woman, smartly dressed, hurried up smiling. "Aunt Fern!" she said. "I'm Eloise Mayo. Remember? You used to let me pick flowers in your yard. I haven't been back here in years, and now everyone's old except you. How did you do it? You look terrific!"

Mayo? Fern thought. Where was her mind? She couldn't place this girl, but she did remember as in a dream, children picking flowers in her yard.

Careful not to stand on anyone's grave, people lingered to visit, catching up on news since last they met. Anecdotes and memories brought sudden bursts of laughter, quickly subdued out of respect for the setting. But tears got no farther than anyone's lashes. The funeral was over. They were all still alive except Sadie.

Fern had become separated from Maude Ellen, whose circle of friends was always different from her own. In the thinning crowd, she now spotted Maude up ahead, talking to a woman in a wide-brimmed black hat.

"I'll never forget your sister," the woman said, when Fern came up to join them. "She saved my life, years ago. She's the best nurse in the world."

"I know." Fern looked fondly at Maude Ellen. "I agree." When the woman moved on, she lowered her voice. "Who was that?"

"I've no idea," said Maude Ellen.

"Should we try to speak to the family?"

Maude Ellen studied the number of people already waiting. "No," she said, stepping around a tombstone as she turned to go. "I think they've had enough for today."

As before, they waited in the old Dodge until most of the cars had gone on, down the narrow gravel road that circled in and out of the cemetery. Back at the church, where her own car was parked, Fern continued to sit with Maude Ellen in hers.

"I hardly shed a tear today, Maude," she said. "And I usually cry more than anybody. What's wrong with me?"

"Nothing," said Maude Ellen. "Death gets old, like anything else. Besides, what was there to cry about? Sadie lived a long time and had a good life. It would have all been downhill from now on. I hope I get to go the same way."

"Not me," said Fern. "I hope I get a little warning!"

Cars pulled up and people got out, going their separate ways. Women came out of the church carrying flowers. A man who looked like a deacon closed the big double doors and locked them from outside, with what seemed an oversized key.

"Well, I guess I better go." Fern sighed, and reached for the handle to the door.

"I'm glad about the man," Maude Ellen said, unexpectedly. "Is he nice?"

"Yes." Fern stopped, her hand on the door. "He's wonderful. It's just so late in the day for me now. And before, you know . . ."

"Forget that," Maude Ellen said. "That's over and done. History." A grin spread over the frown on her face. "You'll have somebody to ride off in the sunset with you!"

Fern leaned over and kissed her on the cheek, a cheek like doeskin in the gloves they used to wear.

As she drove through town, things were almost back to normal. Several stores had closed for the funeral, but people were now back on the street, the women still dressed up, the men in coats and ties. A black bow was on the door of Ainsworth's, the department store started by Sadie's husband's father, years ago. Around the corner, Robert's old dental office had been remodeled. The gingerbread porch was gone, the outside covered in blue aluminum siding.

From the main street, Fern turned west and headed home. When she unlocked her back door, the phone was ringing. That would be Charles, who'd been calling, checking, waiting, and she hurried through the kitchen to answer.

There on the counter was his cake. On the footed glass stand, it was under cover now, but she knew how it looked under there. Pristine white over that dark chocolate heart, as tempting as when she'd made it. She hadn't taken his cake to Sadie's, after all. There'd been enough desserts, and cakes of all kinds, without it.

Swing Low: A Memoir

His name was William Edwards (pronounced Ed'ards by black people on the farm) and he cleaned up our house. Winter and summer he came to work in baggy serge pants and a sagging Sunday coat handed down from my father. With a bustling air of importance and a quick "hidy, hidy" to Joanna, the cook, he arrived like a country preacher entering his church.

He called my mother Miss, like all black people on the place, and she was his boss, though in a way they were workers together, since they had the same lord and master, my father. My mother called my father Mister Ward, which was customary in the rural tradition in which she was raised, but a large part of the deference seemed to be her own. In return, he addressed her as sweetheart (pronounced sweedart), no matter where or when.

Though she was his boss, my mother worked longer and harder than William, since she had two jobs. She ran the store, a farm commissary that stocked everything from groceries to bolts of cloth and horse collars, and she tried to run our house. In the store she kept books for the whole plantation-style operation and, with the help of one black clerk, Bob Spencer, waited on trade from whatever hour of winter or summer daylight arrived until it ended and the 'hands' came in for the night. On Sunday, together with William and Joanna, she tried to put our house in order, and that was the day William usually showed up half-drunk or hung over.

Sunday after Sunday, she would get up early and make a tour of the house, putting cross marks with her finger on dusty surfaces, checking under beds, spotting cobwebs in corners. When William arrived, a little late and reeking, but in a great, optimistic hurry, they could soon be heard behind some open door.

"I told you last week," she would say, "not to let my house get like this again, and here it is as bad as ever." She would pause. "So I'll have to tell him. I'll just say, 'Mr. Ward, you'll have to send William back to the field, and let me have somebody I can depend on.'"

There would be a short, wounded silence, interrupted by a sniffle. Half-drunk and hung over, he could always muster up a few rheumy tears.

"Miss," he would say, "I want to ast you something. Could you be that hard on your old po' nigger?"

It always seemed to work. Her voice would emerge in another defeat. "All right, get the dust rag and dust the legs of that table. Then take the polish and polish it, please."

Before either of them could get on with William's weekly second chance, however, another crisis usually arose. My father did not work on Sunday morning but read the newspaper, smoked a cigar, and went to Sunday School instead. In the small country church we attended, he was not only Superintendent of the Sunday School but teacher of the Adult Class as well. He took his duties seriously when the time came, but not before. His lessons were prepared minutes in advance and began with the finding of the Sunday School book.

"William," he would call out around nine o'clock. "Where's my Sunday School book?"

"I don't know, sir, Mister Wa'd. I ain't seed it."

"Ain't seed it? Why the hell ain't you seed it? Don't you clean up?"

"Yes, sir, but . . ."

Beneath my father's blue-grey eyes, one of which was crossed, the search would begin, through stacks of newspapers and farm magazines, the drawers of tables. The book was wherever my father had left it the Sunday before, in the store, the car, sometimes the church itself. But he never looked for the book himself. Household crises were not his concern. He only looked at the people who were supposed to look.

"Hurry up, dammit."

My father had no patience whatsoever. Having lost his own father at the age of eleven and, with little further schooling or support of any kind except the prayers of his mother, he'd started out at odd jobs in his home county, one of small farms worked by their owners. Little by little, he'd made his way to the rich Black Belt where he'd managed to build the world in which we all now lived. His calculating intelligence and driving energy were never turned off except during sleep. His coat pockets bulged with letters, kept not for matters inside, but for columns of figures running up and down the backs and fronts of their envelopes. Hasty blocks of addition and subtraction identified magazines and newspapers that he'd read. Whether from habit or heredity, he was unable to relax and wait for anything, large or small, to happen. On Sunday mornings he sat in the living room, paring and scraping his nails with a black-handled pocket knife from the store, a small but unnerving sound. Search for the book moved upstairs.

"William?" he would call out. "You got it?"

"No, sir. Not yit."

"Well hurry up, dammit," he'd call louder. "I won't even have time to read over the lesson!"

At this point William would think of something. My father had a boss too, the God of the Baptists, who turned away His face from drinking, dancing, card playing, and profanity. William would reappear, still without the book.

"Mister Wa'd, let me ast you somethin'," he would say. "What good do it do you, cussin' and gwine to church all at the same time? Don't you know somebody up there writing down all them hells and damns you be sayin'?"

My father's religion was so simple it bordered on superstition. It was not a thing to which he gave much thought. In his teeming brain, it was synonymous with the literal Bible, an authority he had no time to read, much less question. William was right, he must have thought. He wanted as few black marks against him as possible on the Day of Judgment.

"Well, y'all run me crazy," he said one Sunday morning. "Jesus Christ would cuss."

My mother was the one who found the book, brought my father a tie, and soothed him on his way. Then, with William sobered up beside her, they started on the house.

William's fingers appeared to be blunt and clumsy but were surprisingly careful. He didn't drop or break objects when dusting. He could lift heavy furniture and heft it about a room, scrub and wax floors on his knees, wash windows to shining clarity. My mother didn't have him do these things on Sunday mornings, however. She only set things straight and primed him for the upcoming week.

One of his merits as a cleaner was his conversation as they worked side by side. An inveterate gossip, he told her things that, as farm mistress, she needed to know.

"You know that little yellow gal fell out in the field yistiddy?" He would flick the rungs of a chair with a brown feather duster. "She didn't have no spell, like they say. She in a family way."

They usually wound up in warm rapport about the time my father got back from church and from visiting with neighbors in the church yard. Occasionally, before coming home, he had to open up the store for someone, which sabotaged his Christianity until he sat down to fried chicken, rice and cream gravy, or baked hen with cornbread dressing.

"You do such good work when you try," my mother would tell William as they finished up, watering potted ferns on stands in front of the living room windows.

"Well, you learnt me," he would say. "Wadn't for you, I'd be ignorant as everybody else on this place."

He would hang up his feather duster and put away the dust mop, dust rag, and red furniture polish. Then he'd go to the kitchen and sit down heavily on a straight chair, to wait for Sunday dinner.

Joanna would be frying chicken, frying corn, candying sweet potatoes or boiling rice, cooking one or two meats and three or four vegetables, hot bread and dessert, as she did every noon.

"She ought to run you off the place," she would tell him.

"I know it." He'd shake his head. "She got a tender heart, though, thank God."

"I wish somebody would send me to the field," Joanna would say, sweating over the black wood-burning iron stove, summer and winter.

"Go by yourself, then," he'd tell her. "Don't wait for me. Them rows git five miles long befo' sundown. No, God. Let me clean up long as I live."

After Sunday dinner, my parents usually rested on the sleeping porch until three or four o'clock in the afternoon, when they rode around the whole place, which had grown by now to several thousand acres. During the ride, my father often gave my mother a pointed opening.

"William was drunk again, I see."

"No, sir, he was all right. He drinks a little of that cheap wine on Saturday night, but they all do that."

So the Sundays passed into years and William was never sent back to the field, but during my last years of high school his days in our household seemed to be numbered.

My mother had begun to feel the years of hard work and long hours. After a full week in the store, she was worn out on Sunday morning. Also, though no one suspected, she had cancer. Her weekly set-to's with William became more climactic, but she steadfastly refused to have him replaced.

Then came the episode of my father's bottle. Strict Baptist that he was, in his heart my father disapproved of drinking. But the years of struggle and unrelenting responsibility were taking their toll on him as well. His operation now included a cotton gin, saw mill, planer mill, grist mill, blacksmith shop, beef cattle and dairy, besides all the crops. More than two hundred black people lived and worked on the place. He had a succession of overseers, but was driven to oversee everyone and everything himself. On an especially hard day, he began to make quick trips to the house for a few swigs of whiskey straight from the bottle. It soon became obvious that someone else had the same idea.

"I thought there was more in this bottle," he began to say to my mother. Since his trips to the house had no regularity and his drinks were hasty, unmeasured, and quickly forgotten in the press of the day, he first suspected himself. But being by nature deadly accurate (he knew almost to the penny how much money he owed and how much was owed him, how many bales of cotton were made on each plot of land, how many feet of lumber ran through his mill in a week), he was not fooled for long.

"Joanna wouldn't touch it," he reasoned out loud one Saturday night. Joanna had once been in jail for a day and night and was fanatically law abiding. "So it's got to be William. I've been drinking behind that son-of-a-gun all this time!"

"Don't say anything about it, though," he told my mother. "I just want to catch him!"

But first thing next morning, my mother was up confronting William.

"There's no use to deny it," she told him. "You're just going from bad to worse. What on earth is to become of you?"

This was beyond tricks or cajolery, he knew. "All right, Miss." He held up both hands as if to ward off the rest. "You don't have to say no more."

The whiskey level didn't recede again, but something else always seemed to be missing. Pecans from the back porch, sausage from the smoke house. A scuttle of coal was mysteriously emptied. We kept running out of Lifebuoy soap.

"That old rogue," my father said.

My mother never failed to defend him. "But he leaves in broad daylight," she would say. "Empty-handed."

Meanwhile William grew thin and quiet. His good, hard-working wife had died, and he was courting a young woman on another place. It was news he neglected to tell my mother, who heard it from Joanna instead. His gal was making a fool of him, Joanna said. She didn't love him because he was too old and, besides, there was nothing to her. All she was, was gimme, gimme. He'd already given her everything he had, even some of the quilts pieced by his dead wife.

As if to bring the whole thing to a head, one of my brothers came home for a quick visit. Ours was a mixed-up family. My mother was a young widow with a small son at the time she married my father, divorced and with a son the same age as her own. It was a case of my child, your child, and our child, with seventeen years between. Neither of my half-brothers had ever lived or worked on the farm, except briefly, however. The ins and outs of the situation had separated us, though not in kinship, early on. It was now my mother's son, living in Chicago and working his way through law school at night, who came home for a few days and missed ten dollars from a wallet left in his room.

My father might not have known but for Joanna, who considered herself under suspicion and meant to establish her innocence where it mattered most.

"God knows I ain't seed it," she said to my father, after the noon meal next day.

"Seed what?" asked my father, and the cat was out of the bag.

The morality of stealing in our house was ambiguous. To take flour, sugar, lard, and such necessities, was overlooked and even expected, but money was not to be touched. Small change and pennies were supposed to lie around indefinitely in ash trays or on the tops of dressers. "He wouldn't take a penny," was the ground rule for honesty.

My father was not one to avoid embarrassing or awkward situations. His aim was not to please but to keep the farm going and solve its problems. He brought this one up at the first opportunity, which was the next meal.

"All right," he announced, as soon as he'd served his plate. "This thing with William has gone too far."

"I'll see him first thing in the morning," my mother said.

"I'll see him myself," my father overruled.

Always first up in the morning, my mother was downstairs before daylight to meet William. She had a fire going in the breakfast-room fireplace when he got there, and she called him in at once. Still in her long woolen bathrobe, her very looks must have told him what was coming.

"Have you still got the money?" she asked.

He shook his head, then eased over to the fireplace and held out one hand to the warmth of the blaze. My mother poked the coals and said nothing. Darkness blacked out the windows, and a lone Delco light bulb, suspended on a cord from the ceiling, lit the room like a wan Last Judgment.

"You might as well go on back home then, I guess." She put the poker back in its wrought-iron stand and turned to face him.

He started to leave without a word, but she stopped him at the door. "Why didn't you ask me for the money?"

"You wouldn't of let me had it," he said.

"Mr. Ward is really mad this time," she said. "I don't know what he'll do."

"Well, that's all right, Miss," he told her. "I don't belong to Mr. Wa'd like the rest of these niggers. I belongs to you. You done told me what to do."

He took his hat from a crisscross folding hat rack in the kitchen where it always hung. Joanna was making up biscuits. Smoked bacon was frying, coffee perking. Joanna didn't speak or even look at him. He'd put her back in the shadow of a jail, she felt, and she wanted no part of him.

It was a cold morning, my mother said later, and his skin had a whitish cast as if the frost had bit it. She thought his coat was too thin for the weather. She stood by the fire for a minute, then went to get dressed and open up the store, to see the hands off to work as usual.

If my mother had ever used artifice, even in appearance, she'd given it up by now. In girlhood she'd been considered pretty, and her good looks endured in straight features, clear olive complexion, and expressive dark eyes. But she'd become too stout. She wore her hair short and straight because it was no trouble, used no cosmetics except face powder, owned no clothes except the plainest of work dresses and one or two, hastily bought on rare trips to town, for Sundays and funerals. Except for the cameo she usually wore, the few pieces of jewelry she owned were in the lock box of a bank. She didn't know how to be deceptive.

"The money's back," she told my father at the dinner table that day, in what was meant to be an off-hand manner.

"What do you mean, back?" he asked.

She took a heavy envelope from her sweater pocket and handed it over. My father glanced at the dollar bills, the quarters and half dollars weighing down the envelope, and gave it back to her.

"Looks like some of your egg money to me," he said.

My mother said nothing.

"We can't have stealing in the house, sweedart," he said. "You can't abet a thing like that. I'm surprised at you."

My mother's face flushed all the way down to her neck. "It won't happen again," she said.

Years later, old, lonely, unhappy in a disastrous third marriage, my father liked to talk about my mother when he had a secret chance. "She was too good for her own good," he would say. Then looking off into space, he'd add with a sigh, "Still, she was no reed shaken with the wind."

My mother was right about William. Things stopped disappearing after that. His young gal had quit him for some other fool, Joanna reported, and it was no longer "hidy, hidy" when he came to work. He was in and out like a shadow, polite but distant, his face a mask.

"What's eating on him?" my father wanted to know.

"He's just sad," my mother said. "He'll be all right."

"Sad?" My father shook his head. Only Negroes and irresponsible people had time to be sad, he probably thought at the time. As for himself, he was too busy.

When William recovered, he was changed for the better. My

mother no longer smelled whiskey on his breath on Sunday mornings. There were no dust balls under beds or cobwebs in corners. With his busy feather duster, dust rag trailing from a sagging hip pocket, he was someone to depend on at last. My mother began going to church with my father.

Like most people absorbed in work that they love, my mother had few physical complaints. She'd always been strong and healthy, so people leaned on her, both black and white. Her health seemed all of a piece with her character, which we took for granted. When she began to have symptoms no one knew, because she didn't tell us.

It was not until she began to be wakeful at night that the fact was forced upon my father.

"What's wrong?" he would ask, hearing her up.

"Taking an aspirin," she would say. "Go back to sleep."

It was some time before he thought to ask, "Aspirin for what?"

Her trouble came from standing and walking all day, she said. Always at hand was what she called her "doctor box," equipped from years of doctoring people on the place. My father couldn't afford to call the country doctor, who was also a friend, for the minor complaints of so many people, so my mother had of necessity become a kind of plantation nurse. Someone was always on our back porch, it seemed, soaking a hand or foot in a strong solution of carbolic acid and near-scalding water. She kept gauze and adhesive tape, rubbing alcohol, iodine, laxatives, ear drops and toothache drops, stomach medicine, diuretics, and a variety of pain killers. Now she doctored herself, and it was not until she began to lose weight noticeably that she told the doctor her symptoms.

From the first examinations, we heard the chilling phrase "too late," but always with a could-be or might-be. The hysterectomy was quick and decisive.

The black women cried out loud when they heard it. "Oh, Lord, help us," they sobbed. "Jesus, have mercy."

On summer nights, as we lay in our beds with open windows, their laments would often float up from the little one or two-room houses. First a high, clear, lone soprano would throw out a tentative line, which seemed to hang in the air until a listening voice caught it, began to play with it, and a gathering chorus set the beat. The night would then ache with music, half spiritual, half blues, saying that life is hard, almost too hard to bear. A ten-cent harmonica from the store would solo, a male or female voice would take over, and back to the chorus. Finally, abruptly, the soulful pathos would be cut short by a burst of laughter, loose, earthy, and totally free, which spread from yard to yard like rain after heat.

My mother, helped by my brother, made a trip to the Mayo Clinic. She went through a series of X-ray treatments, but had accepted her fate early on.

For a while she dressed and went to the store as usual. Where she'd once stood and walked, she now sat and watched. A cot was set up toward the back, out of sight, so she could rest when the pain pills took over. Confined at last to the house, with William to help, she went through possessions, cleaning out and throwing away or putting up for safekeeping. As long as she was able, she had the farm account books brought to her, and posted them sitting in a pillow-cushioned chair or propped up in bed.

But it was now her turn to lean on someone, and she leaned most on William, who was always there. Joanna went home after the noon meal each day, then came back to put a supper of leftovers on the table and wash up the dishes.

William finished his regular housework by noon, but began staying on of his own accord, sitting in the kitchen, usually head in hands, waiting for my mother's little hand-bell to tinkle. Later on a practical nurse, then a trained nurse were brought in to take care of her, but William stayed on as well.

"You better go on home and try to get something done," my father would tell him, since everyone sharecropped on the side.

"Miss might want something," he would say, and go on sitting, waiting for some small errand such as a trip to the store, the need for a tablespoon or the squeezing of a lemon. In cool weather he kept the fires going, not too hot and not too cool, fussing over grates and coal-burning heaters like a living thermostat.

He took it upon himself to answer the back door, since black women came up every day to see my mother. Most came out of concern, but some were simply idle and curious and William weeded them out at a glance.

"She sleep," he would say, opening the back door and seeing the wrong face. "Ain't no need to wait."

My father couldn't get over it. "William has turned out to be the best old scoundrel I ever saw," he would say, as before a real phenomenon.

My mother must have been lonely. My father was in and out during the day but never for long. He was without his good right hand and had to compensate as best he could. I was away at school, not far, but away. My mother wouldn't hear to my coming home. She was determined that I have the education she had missed. My brother was hundreds of miles away.

We were called home for the last week of her life, which was spent in a deepening coma. Once, at the beginning of the end, she came to unexpectedly and was lucid. My father, my brother, and I were hurried into the room. William and Joanna stood outside in the hall.

"I must have been asleep," my mother said in a vague, apologetic voice. "Is it night or day?"

"It's day, sweedart," my father said, leaning over the bed. "Ten o'clock in the morning."

She looked curiously from one face to the other, and we all moved closer, hoping to be recognized or even spoken to.

An unmistakable sob from the hall interrupted. Someone hurried to close the door, but my mother had heard.

"Was that William?" she asked, and called out weakly, "William . . .?"

We moved aside to let him come, weeping without restraint, while all that was left of her seemed to focus on his grief.

"Poor William," she said. "Don't cry . . ."

But it was too much for her. She frowned, shut her eyes, and turned her head. My brother led William from the room.

The funeral was held at home as she would have liked. The house was thoroughly clean and in order. Friends had filled it with flowers. The short service, led by our country preacher, was attended by so many people they had to stand outside, all over the front yard and into the road. The newspaper obituary referred to my mother as a "beloved woman."

There was no music during the service. But at its close, a group of black singers, self-selected as the best on the place, stood outside under the carport and sang "Swing Low, Sweet Chariot" as they brought the casket out.

Joanna, William, and Bob were to ride with the family to the cemetery. A farm truck was to bring any of the rest who wanted to come. But when it was time to leave, William couldn't be found, so we had to go on without him.

It was not until we got home that we found him alone in the back yard, sitting in a chair under the trees.

"She gone," he announced, when we went up to ask him what happened, and why he hadn't gone with us. "I ain't got nobody now."

My father went up and patted him awkwardly on the shoulder. "You got us," he said.

William looked at my father as if to say You? Then his eyes filled with large tears that began to roll down his cheeks, and onto his clean, white, Sunday shirt.

"Nobody," he repeated. "Not in this world."

Alone in a Foreign Country

HER NAME WAS CATHY. She was from Mississippi and this was Moscow, six thousand miles from home. Her Daddy had found out from the airlines before she left. "Too far," he kept saying. "Too far!" She was twenty-three, and hadn't been out of the States before.

Now, in a dark hotel room, in the middle of the night, something at the door had waked her. She turned on her back so as to hear with both ears, but heard nothing. She raised her head up from the pillow and listened. Nothing. Had she dreamed it?

Her room was down a long dimly lit hall, so long and dim, with shadowy turns on the worn patterned carpet, that she always felt uneasy toward the end. She'd been late, almost too late, to sign up, so had to be tacked on as a single.

"Think you'll be okay?" Dr. Gilmore, head of the group, had asked, as they settled in after midnight the night before.

"Oh, yes, sir." Actually, she'd have felt better with a roommate like everyone else, but would never have said so. She didn't want to be a problem in any way.

"Keep your door locked."

"Yes, sir. I will."

Her group, English teachers here for credit, was smaller than she'd expected and mostly middle-aged women. Beverly, from St. Louis, was young, but with a two-year-old daughter at home. Divorced since last fall, she'd said on the plane, growing quiet and staring out the window at clouds. Now it was May, with lilacs in bloom over here.

Cathy was a teacher in the high school at home, but different from the rest of the group, she thought. She didn't want to be a teacher forever. What she wanted to be was a wife and mother, in a marriage that lasted a lifetime. She'd rather stay at home and keep house, cook hot suppers. But she hadn't yet met the right man.

One of her reasons for coming on this trip (though she wouldn't want anyone to know) was the hope that he would be in the group. Someone nice, literary, close to a doctorate, maybe. Someone who cared about something besides football. In daydreams she was always an English professor's wife.

But the only two men near her age were a couple, traveling together. Another man, not too old but married, was companion to his father, an aging scholar whose side he never left. So she'd enjoy the trip and keep looking.

They'd had a full first day, plus a long evening lecture on Pushkin, so she'd been counting on a good night's sleep to be up and ready in the morning. Beverly was to knock on her door before breakfast and a day on the tour bus.

Ah! She caught her breath in the darkness. There was the sound again, just outside her door. Small, sneaky, like the gnawing of a rat in a wall, like someone fiddling with the lock on her door. And definitely real, no dream. She propped up on an elbow to listen, became a pinpoint of listening.

She could see in her mind the deadlock on her door, its iron bolt securely in place. She'd checked it again before getting in bed, to be sure. The lock couldn't be picked, she knew, but there were other keys, not just the one with the heavy room tag on the table by her bed. The housekeeper would have one, plus maids, and who knew who else.

She eased up in bed to find the light switch, and a small bedside lamp lit the room like a candle. The big room, square and old-fashioned, with its high ceiling and oblong bathroom set into one quarter, was more like a guestroom in a once-fine residence than a leading Moscow hotel. In the corner next to the bathroom wall, her narrow bed was set apart, canopied in shadows, its twin on the opposite side of the room.

When the sound came again she slipped out of bed and crept barefoot to the door, where she squatted with her ear to the lock. In a moment the door rattled. She could feel it. So someone was there fooling with the lock. No question.

She hurried back to sit trembling on the bedside, trying to think what to do. She couldn't scream for help over here, not in the middle of the night. Naturally shy, then baptized in Southern manners, she'd never caused a disturbance anywhere in her life. And she couldn't wake up Dr. Gilmore or anyone in the group. She hardly knew them. Also, they were tired and jetlagged. She didn't know how they'd react.

But she could call the desk, and ask for someone to come and check it out. They wouldn't mind and, besides, it was their job.

The phone was on a desk across the room, and on the way she held her breath. She hadn't used the phone since she got here, hadn't found out how to use it, hadn't even paid attention to complaints from the group.

Numbers on the dial were Arabic, but everything else was in Russian and beyond her. She picked up the receiver and got no dial tone, but dialed zero anyway and got dead plastic. With a shaky forefinger, gone strangely numb, she jiggled the prongs and dialed again. Nothing.

She checked the cord and connections, dialed numbers, letters, symbols, with no success. She held down the prongs and released them, dialed zero again. Nothing.

So the phone wasn't working, like many Russian facilities, or she didn't know how to work it. She dialed 911, just in case, and gave up. Like a benched athlete, she went back to her bed and sat down.

Meanwhile, the sound came and went unpredictably. A quick shake-shake-shake, then silence. The silence between rattles was sometimes short, sometimes so long she began to have hope. But the door always rattled as before.

Whoever was there would get in, she was sure. He'd have tools as well as keys, and would try until something worked. "If they want to get in, they will," she'd heard people say all her life.

Barefoot, in a gown that took up no more luggage room than a rolled-up pair of socks, she shook as from a chill. Her hands and feet were icy, her mouth dry. From time to time, she thought she felt a draft in the room but, focused on the door, she ignored it.

If she'd listened to her Daddy she wouldn't be here, she thought. He'd opposed this trip from the start.

"Why Russia?" he kept saying. "You know it's not safe. Why would anybody get up such a trip in the first place?"

But she'd been determined to come. She loved Russian literature and wanted to see the land of the great Russian writers. And she'd thought, however foolishly, she'd meet a man who was right for her. It was the chance of a lifetime, she'd thought.

Next time, though, she would listen. And when she got home she'd stay there. She'd be a good teacher and leave the rest to fate.

But a radical thought suddenly shot through her brain. What if she never got home, never got out of this room alive?

The skin on her arms prickled as stories of girls robbed, raped, and murdered scrolled before her as on a screen. Their faces before the tragedies were always smiling.

Whoever was there could have her money. Dollars, credit cards, all. She'd hand it over in a heartbeat. But rape? She hadn't saved herself all this time for some thug, probably with AIDS. It would ruin her whole life and her dreams. She'd never get over it even if she lived, so she'd fight to the end. He'd have to kill her.

But, dear God in Heaven, she didn't want to die. She wasn't ready! She'd been like a flower by the roadside or a leaf on a tree, not realizing she was living any more than they did.

The door rattled harder, faster. She shut her eyes and tried to pray, "Help me, save me!" But her connection to God was like the one on the phone. She didn't know how to work it. Crying, but not wanting to be heard, she let tears roll down her cheeks and fall on her gown in silence. Over her heart, the gown pulsed. The room, which had been comfortable before, was now drafty and cold.

Like answered prayer, an idea came as on a flash card. If she could hold out until morning, people would be up and down the hall, and whoever was there would have to leave. Beverly would come, and he'd be gone.

She was up at once as if ejected, pushing furniture against the door. First she pushed up the table from which she'd moved the phone, then a big upholstered chair. Like a school janitor, she pushed up a writing desk, a heavy wooden luggage bench, another chair. She unplugged a lamp, set it on a table for its crash value, stacked a small chair on top of a big one.

With everything against the door except the beds and TV, she leaned against the wardrobe to catch her breath, and a sudden sweet breeze cooled her damp back and shoulders. Like summertime at home, she thought, with quick longing.

But where did the breeze come from? Windows in the room were all shut, she remembered. She'd tried to open one and been told they were closed for warmth all winter, and not yet opened up for spring.

She checked sashes behind draperies and found them secure. Yet air came in, in waves. It blew on her shoulders and stirred her loose hair. She stood mystified until she looked up.

Above the windows was an old-fashioned transom, something she hadn't noticed at all. And the transom was partially open, so that wind, when it blew, could come through.

Was it only the wind, then, that had rattled her door? A diabolical trick, or joke? The rattle had waxed and waned, it was true, had come and gone as it listed. And she hadn't heard it since she first pushed a table against the door. Had she simply propped the door so tight it couldn't rattle?

Feeling weak, she went back to her bed and sat down. The room was quiet, the rattle gone. Her watch, on the floor beside the bed, said five o'clock. But darkness didn't reach Moscow until after eleven at night, so morning was still a long way off here.

She lay down, stretched out, and gave a deep sigh. It was not a sigh of relief, however, only respite. She was safe for the night, she supposed, but sometime, somewhere, her time would come.

And what then? The question had prowled around her consciousness before. But safe at home, she'd shut it out.

Would she be blotted out and simply not be? Go back to the nothingness from which she'd been born? The steady little flame that was her self would go out, and darkness would descend forever. For infinity!

Her mind reeled away from the thought. Her heart was like a woodchopper at work in her chest. She thought she couldn't breathe and needed more air, but knew she couldn't open a window. Sat up and put her feet on the floor, as if to escape.

One of her students, Marilyn, had panic attacks. To understand and maybe help, she'd once asked Marilyn what it was that she feared. "Everything!" Marilyn had said in a thin little whisper, and began to cry so she couldn't go on.

What she meant was death, Cathy understood now. Death had to be the root, the taproot, of fears. For everything else there was hope of some cure, reprieve, degree of improvement, or the power of endurance, at least. But death!

To stop shivering, she got between the sheets and pulled up the covers, the extra blanket. She'd never been so tired in her life, she thought, and buried her head in pillows. Her nerves seemed to vibrate like roadside power lines at home. All of her muscles ached. So she'd get warm and rest for a minute, then move a few things back in place.

When she opened her eyes it was daylight, and someone was knocking on the door. She was up at once, climbing over furniture, pulling things out of the way.

"Beverly?" she called, through the crack she'd just made. "I thought someone was trying to get in my room last night. I overslept."

"Oh?" She could see Beverly staring wide-eyed at the barricade she'd put up.

"So I'm not ready." She pushed back the hair falling in her face. "I can't make it to breakfast, but I'll see you at the bus."

Fresh and rested, ready for the day, Beverly looked back through the crack. "See you later then," she said, and went off down the hall.

Was Beverly trying not to smile? Cathy thought. Did she think it was funny?

She had to put back furniture now, before she left. The bus would be gone all day, and she didn't want the maids to see what she'd done. But it was harder to put back than to move in the night, and she worked like a dreamer muddling through a dream.

When she looked at her watch again, still in her gown, she had fifteen minutes to get on the bus.

This was the day they would visit Chekhov's house and hear talks by Chekhov scholars. She'd looked forward to this day more than any. Now, above all, she didn't want to be left behind, alone in a foreign city. What happened in the night was still in her mind like a lash in the eye. Back with the group, she'd feel safe, she thought.

She splashed water on her face and threw on clothes. Without looking in a mirror, she ran down the hall.

On the bus, fortified with coffee and big Russian breakfasts, everyone was waiting as she ran up the steps out of breath. From every seat, sleep-rested faces looked at her, each one holding something back, it seemed, something not related to her lateness. When she paused to look for a seat, one of the women spoke out.

"We heard you had an adventure last night," she said, in a teasing way.

Adventure? Cathy's smile of apology faded.

"Did you think there was a man at your door?" asked a woman from the Midwest, eyes twinkling beneath satiny green lids.

Chuckles scattered from seat to seat.

Cathy spotted an empty seat near the back of the bus and hurried down the aisle past everyone, past Beverly, grinning with the rest. At the window, she stared blindly out.

She didn't turn her head when Beverly slid into the seat beside her. Beverly leaned closer and whispered in her ear.

"Cathy," she said. "They were teasing, you know. We've all been there ourselves, one way or another, scared to death over nothing. You have to forget it. Tomorrow you'll laugh about it!"

Laugh? Cathy turned back to the window. Forget?

The bus made a ponderous turn, gave a beast-like groan, and moved into the main city traffic. She looked out at golden domes, statues, formal beds of flowers. Overnight, the scene looked different, unreal and unsettling. And on the street, people hurried along like figures in a dream.

But on the bus, everyone was looking out windows or chatting as usual. Did they know? she wondered. If so, how could they be so unconcerned?

Beside her, Beverly opened a tote bag stored at her feet. From inside she brought out a large glazed bun, loosely wrapped in coarse Russian paper.

"I thought you might be hungry," she said, "with no breakfast." She handed the bun to Cathy with a smile.

Cathy took the bun and thanked her, but held it. "I was terrified last night," she said. "For a while, I thought I wouldn't even be here today."

"But you are," Beverly said. "So you can forget it. Right?"

Cathy shook her head. "I don't think so, no. I'd never faced death at all until last night." She looked directly at Beverly. "Have you, ever?"

"Look!" Beverly took charge as in a classroom. "We're here on vacation, more or less, aren't we? The scare is over and you're okay. This stuff is morbid, so let's drop it and enjoy ourselves. All right?"

Cathy began to eat. The bun was good, hearty, like all Russian breads, like the people who'd once turned back Hitler.

"Thanks again," she said, when she'd finished. She brushed crumbs from her jeans, used one of the Russian words that she'd learned. "Spasjiba!"

Strange. Before she came, she'd read about Tolstoy and his night at Arzamus. A thought, not a sound, had caused his terror at the inn. It was the thought of his own death, whenever that might be. He'd waked up his servant and ordered a coach, to get him away from Arzamus. While waiting, he'd fallen asleep until morning, but he was never to get over that night. It would haunt and affect him for the rest of his days, would change his whole life and his art.

The bus shuddered and came to a stop. They'd reached the home of Chekhov. The house had been too small for him and his large, financially dependent family, so he'd called it "the chest of drawers." Vintage Chekhov, someone said.

Everyone began to get out. The male couple stood back courteously for her to go first. The woman from the Midwest winked fraternally when they met in the aisle. But Beverly pushed on ahead. When Cathy looked for her outside, she was way up front with the tour guide, facing the other way.

The House That Asa Built

NORTH CREEK LIFE was hard in Alabama in the nineteen fifties, but Pearl Oakes was happy. She had Asa and the children, her own little house, a good stove and refrigerator. The only thing she needed and lacked was a washing machine. Asa was to get that in town today, by means of the installment plan.

To celebrate, Pearl had everything ready for when he got home. A baked hen was in the warming oven, cooked vegetables on the stove, and two pecan pies in the kitchen safe. She'd dressed up the beds with quilts that she'd made, had hung freshly ironed towels on the towel racks, and had put on her prettiest housedress.

Danny and Sister were playing on the woodpile, lost in the freedom of Saturday afternoon. They'd had all-over baths, and their heads were like two pale dandelions, the clean, straight hair ready to fly away with a good puff of wind.

From their small front porch, Pearl watched the narrow road that wound out of sight through October woods. Asa would be back any minute now, she thought, so when a red pickup truck came in sight, she let it pass without interest. Her eyes were on the hills beyond for Asa's wagon.

The thought of a washing machine was like Christmas in child-hood to her. She didn't mind washing and took pride in hanging a clean wash on the line, but carrying water to the wash pot and stooping over the rub board had come to make her back ache. She told Asa last year, but he bought a set of the World Book Encyclopedia instead.

"We can't let the children come up like we did, Pearl," he said. "It wouldn't be right."

Asa's lack of education was the regret of his life. Still, he was an independent farmer who'd never worked for anyone else a day in his life, and she thought that was something. It was his secret pride too, though he'd never say so. Asa wasn't like other men and she'd known it from the start. After ten years of marriage, he was still a mystery to her at times.

She was surprised when the red truck turned into their yard and drove up to the house. MOORE'S FURNITURE AND APPLIANCE was lettered on the door. A white man leaned from the window of the cab.

"Asa Oakes live here?" he asked.

"Yes, sir," she said cautiously.

"We brought his television set," the man said.

Pearl saw a brown television braced against the cab of the truck. A colored boy rose from where he sat folded beside it. The white man got out and slammed the truck door.

"It don't belong here, though," Pearl said quickly. "I don't know where it's supposed to go."

"Asa Oakes just bought it, ma'am," the man said, and went around to help the colored boy unload it.

Danny and Sister had come to lean against Pearl, breathing like excited young animals.

"He went to get a washing machine," she said in a thin voice, as the two men eased their delivery onto the porch.

The white man looked at her, shook his head. "Well," he said, "this'll give you more pleasure out here. This'll be a heap of company for you all. Where do you want it put?"

Where? It was the only television set she'd ever seen outside of a store window. She'd meant to put the washing machine here on the porch. Asa said that only country people put washing machines on the front porch, and she'd said, "Well, that's what we are, idn't it? Country people."

"I couldn't say," she told the man. "There's just two rooms and a kitchen, until we build on."

She led the way inside for him to look around. Two beds and a chifforobe filled up the childrens' room. In the other room, the big room, the double bed she shared with Asa sat cater-cornered on a blue linoleum rug. A sofa and overstuffed chair were carefully fitted around it. She'd washed and ironed the curtains when she did fall cleaning, had made new cushion-covers for the straight chairs.

"Over here?" the man asked, from a space at the foot of the bed. "Some people like to watch it at night, in the bed."

"Yes, sir," she said, and backed out of the room.

The colored boy passed her with a box of tools.

She waited on the porch to be out of the way, so she saw Asa's wagon when it first came in sight. He was standing up driving at a trot, and for the first time she watched him with a cold heart. It reduced him to an ordinary man of medium build with thick dark hair. His face, which usually made her think of someone special, a teacher or even preacher, was the face of a plain dirt farmer.

He came toward her first, trying to say something with his eyes. He could tell her things that way as a rule, but not now. She looked back at him as if she'd gone blind, so he touched the heads of his children and hurried on into the house.

"You didn't beat me much!" she heard him joke to the men.

Pearl walked quickly down the steps, around the house, and toward the woods behind it. The wash pot in the back yard seemed to mock her as she went by. On its three short iron legs, the charred remains of last week's fire still beneath its sooty bottom, it looked bigger, blacker, more permanent than ever.

At the edge of the woods, she sat down on a log with her back to the house. Long ago, when she'd been punished as a child (not often, because she'd been good), she'd go outside when it was over, look up at the sky, listen to the birds, and stay out until she recovered. If her feelings were hurt at school, she'd come home, put up her books, and do the same. At sixteen, when she married Asa and moved to this little house he'd built for them by hand, she'd come to this very spot when she felt homesick or sad. In a little while she usually felt better. But not today. Her heart felt too big in her chest, like something she'd swallowed by mistake. The fall air chilled her, and dead leaves kept falling at her feet.

The sky had turned to gunmetal grey when the red truck started up and drove off. Asa came out and called, as to one of the children late coming in. "Pearl. Oh, Pearl!"

She got up slowly, as if arthritic, and turned toward the house. On the roof there was now a silver pole pierced by silver arrows. The sound of music, laughter, and something like applause came from inside.

Asa hurried to meet her. His face was anxious, but underneath she saw the same excitement she'd seen in her children.

"We need this thing, Pearl," he said quickly. "Can't you see that? It can bring the whole world right here to North Creek!"

He held out his hand but she shrank back, hiding her own behind her.

"Listen to me, now," he said. "The children will learn things they couldn't learn no other way. It'll be like another school for them here at home. For us, too!"

She walked on, bent over as if carrying buckets of water in each hand to the wash pot.

In the kitchen, she turned on a light bulb hanging from the ceiling and untied a cloth from the buttermilk pitcher. She couldn't bring herself to look him in the face.

"Come see it first," he begged. "You'll like it!"

Avoiding his eyes, she began to set the table. He waited for a second, then went back to join the children.

She put four plates on the oilcloth tablecloth, four glasses beside them. She sliced half of the hen, surrounded it with cornbread dressing, and dished up the vegetables. She set out a plate of large roll-like biscuits, fresh-made butter, wild plum preserves, and a jar of pickled peaches, with cloves and cinnamon floating around the sides.

When she was through, she went to the door where Danny and Sister sat upright in their chairs, too engrossed to lean back. Danny rocked slightly back and forth with a galloping horseman on the screen. Asa sat gloomily apart, watching too.

"Supper's ready," she said.

The children seemed not to hear, but Asa stood up at once.

"Your mother said supper!" he said. It was a command.

His blessing was short, not long as usual, and they began to eat in silence. The children picked at their food, though chicken and dressing was their favorite dish. They usually loved her biscuits, but tonight they didn't even eat the one they took.

Danny pushed back his plate "I don't want pie, Mama," he said, and slid from his chair. "I'm full."

Asa turned on him. "What's the matter with you, boy? Talking about 'I'm full!' Say 'Excuse me, please,' like you're supposed to!"

Both children scurried back to start watching again. They already knew how to turn the set on and off.

Pearl took a bite of pie to test it, and put down her fork. Asa ate his whole piece and folded his napkin.

"I'd rather you do anything than pout, Pearl," he said.

She brushed crumbs from the table, dropped them into the slop bucket, and began collecting dishes. She still couldn't look him in the face.

In the next room, there was an abrupt change. After a short, brisk announcement, one voice came through, speaking with authority.

"The world news!" Asa said excitedly. "Now that's worth watching. Come on, Pearl. You ought to see it!"

She turned to the dish pan and he left.

She'd been taught to set the table for breakfast the night before. She set it now, covered it over with a clean white cloth, and went alone to the childrens' room. Shivering in the mild night, she put on her nightgown and got into Sister's bed, on the far side next to the unpainted wall, which still held the faint aromatic fragrance of pine. When the children came in, much later, careful to make no noise, she pretended to be asleep. She'd slept very little when the roosters crowed for day.

On Monday she washed. Tuesday she ironed as usual. It had taken a year to pay for the encyclopedia, and this would take longer, she knew. She cooked each day but couldn't eat what she cooked. She slept by fits and starts. In the mirror of the wash-stand, eyes that seemed starched wide open stared back at her. Asa and the children came and went like phantoms.

Sister leaned against her and played with her fingers. "What's wrong, Mama?" she said. "I love you, Mama."

"What's wrong, Mama?" Danny asked, a worried frown on his face.

Asa stopped trying to win her over and matched silence with silence. She kept her eyes on her work, on the floor, on the space in front of her.

"You're not the only one, Pearl," he finally burst out one day. "I need a tractor bad as you need a washing machine. It takes half my time trying to keep the old one going. We have to put first things first, that's all!"

On Friday morning, she packed a thin suitcase with clothes for herself and the children. In the afternoon, she set out on the kitchen table a platter of fried chicken, a plate of biscuits, baked sweet potatoes, and a fresh pound cake. She put a small portion of each into paper bags for the children, and covered the rest with a cloth for Asa.

When Danny and Sister got off the school bus, she was ready.

"We're going to Aunt Lutie's," she told them. "We have to make haste."

It was four miles to Lutie's, and she meant to be there by dark. She set a rapid pace and kept it, walking steadily. North Creek was hill country, and the road began to seem uphill more than not. Danny and Sister, who'd started out happily, eager to see their cousins, began to lag behind and fret. Pearl shifted the suitcase from one hand to the other.

Now and then the strangeness of leaving Asa burst upon her in a flash of unreality. Has my mind gone bad?, she thought. What am I doing out here with my children? Then she remembered, and hurried on. Dampness rose from the creek bottom and Sister, who was subject to colds, began to cough. The woods seemed to close in darkly.

"We're gettin' closer, though," she told the children, and took Sister by the hand.

Finally, from the top of a hill a light appeared up ahead. It was cozily framed in the window of a house,

"Look, Mama!" Danny shouted. "Look a'yonder!"

The first thing Pearl could make out through the dusk was a solid block of white, a washing machine on the porch. A sense of justification unfurled within her, went up like a banner before her tired senses. She led her children faster up the hill.

Lutie's husband, Buck, opened the door in his sock feet. "Great God A'mighty," he said, when he saw the three of them huddled together in the twilight.

Lutie, drying her hands on a dish towel, came to peer from behind him. Around her, children swirled like a living train.

"My Lord from Zion!" she said, when she saw her sister, "Come on in!"

Lutie, as fat as Pearl was thin, was like a bright balloon blown up too far by a heedless child. Her glad expression changed when she saw Pearl's face. "Why, honey," she said, "What's wrong?"

Pearl lowered her eyes and shook her head. She let the children go in first, then handed Buck the suitcase.

Once inside, she drew a quick breath. "I had a little falling out with Asa," she said.

For a moment, Buck and Lutie looked at her in silence. "I'd a'never thought it of you and Asa," Buck said at last.

Lutie's eyes were like two blue marbles about to be shot from taw. "Well, what on earth did Asa do?" she wanted to know.

For the first time in days, Pearl almost laughed. But the thought of telling, explaining, was too much for her. Her chin began to quiver.

"Skip it and forget it, then!" Lutie said quickly. "We'll have a bite of supper and you'll feel better. I've got it all cooked. Ain't that nice?"

Lutie's house was luxury itself to Pearl. There was an overstuffed living room suite and a big wool rug. The rooms were filled with beds and dressers, tables and chairs. The kitchen, where Lutie now bustled about, had a large stove, refrigerator, and gleaming double sink. But even Lutie had no television.

Lutie dished up a platter of fried ham with red-eye gravy, bowls of grits, butterbeans, and corn. She caught up a plump baby and stuffed her into a high chair, lifted a toddler onto a stool. Last, she brought a plate of biscuits so hot she had to blow on her fingers as she took them from the pan.

"Now help yourself, everybody. There's plenty of it!" she told the crowd around the big kitchen table. Children ranged all the way up to a big adolescent boy.

No one spoke as food began to disappear from plates, platters, bowls. Buck's voice and booming laugh were silenced. So was the childrens' chatter.

Pearl found herself eating too fast like the rest, so she put down her fork and picked up the biscuit plate beside her.

"Have a biscuit, Buck?" she said.

"I'll hep myself," he said shortly.

She couldn't help thinking of Asa. "It gives me the heartburn to eat at Lutie's," he always said. Asa had to have a blessing, then conversation at the table. When Danny ate too fast, he winked at Pearl. "We'll have to get him a trough," he said.

A knock on the door interrupted.

"Now what!" Buck pushed back his chair. No one else stopped eating.

He opened the door and lowered his voice, then stepped outside and pulled the door shut behind him. Lutie got up and brought a deep-dish pie for dessert.

When Buck came back he didn't look at Pearl. On the table in front of Lutie, he laid several bills, neatly folded.

"Asa said he didn't want his family to be a burden on nobody," he said.

"Well, where's Asa at?" Lutie wanted to know.

Buck sat down and adjusted his forearms on the edge of the table. "He went on," he said, and picked up his fork. "He just come to see if his folks was here."

"Now, you know that was nice of Asa," Lutie said.

In bed later, between Danny and Sister, Pearl agreed with Lutie. That was nice of Asa. She followed him guiltily through the dark woods and lonely night until she imagined him nearly home. There she left him, and turned over with a sigh. Almost at once, she was asleep.

When she awoke it was daylight, and Lutie had breakfast on the table.

"I didn't come here to be company," Pearl apologized at once. "I didn't mean to sleep so long."

"Well, I'm proud you did. You look better," Lutie said, and the storm of breakfast was upon them.

This was Saturday, and Buck was in a hurry to get off to town. All of the children were playful. Milk spilled. The baby choked and had to be patted on the back, then held.

"You go on to town with Buck, Sister," Pearl told Lutie. "I'll keep the children. Be glad to."

"No, Lord!" Lutie said. "Not me. Buck won't be back here till midnight."

Pearl couldn't help comparing first one thing, then another. Asa was always home by dark. He had to be there to protect them, he said.

With Buck gone, the children outside, and the baby in bed with a bottle, Lutie glanced over her ravaged table.

"Let's have us a cup of coffee in peace," she said to Pearl, pushing aside dirty dishes. She filled their cups and sat down heavily.

"I know you wonder what I aim to do," Pearl said at once. This was the first chance they'd had to talk since she got here. "I thought I'd go on to Papa's and get work. I can make a living there at the factory."

"Well, Papa needs somebody with him, all right," Lutie said. "He's old and forgetful. Stumbles all around. But I still can't get over it . . . You and Asa!"

"I know." Pearl glanced out the window. Danny and Sister stood off to one side, watching Lutie's children roughhouse over a football.

"Just don't make no mistake," Lutie said, "and do something you can't undo."

Outside, the spirit of play exploded all at once. Lutie's oldest boy and girl flew at each other, faces distorted and lips drawn back. From a deadlock, the girl pulled wildly loose and with animal swiftness sank her teeth into her brother's hand. At the same time, he raised his knee and shoved it deep into her stomach.

Lutie ran out, flowered housecoat belled out around her. The girl had crumpled to her knees, sobbing and holding her stomach.

"I'll get her," the boy said loudly, his voice quivering. "I'll fix her yet!" He held up a hand that bore the exact red and white impression of his sister's teeth.

"You get in the house on that bed," Lutie ordered the girl. "You're all right."

Sobbing loudly, holding her stomach, the girl rushed through the kitchen past Pearl. A door slammed, but loud sobs kept coming through.

Pearl's hands trembled as she tempered water at the sink and began to wash dishes. Stacks of plates and glasses, cups and saucers, black iron skillets to be wiped out but not washed.

"They'll run you crazy!" Lutie said, coming back out of breath.

"Yes, but are you sure she's not hurt?" Pearl asked.

"No, she's not hurt." Lutie picked up a dish towel. "She's as tough as they come. She's a biter, been one all of her life. Sometimes she draws blood. I've done everything I can, and can't break her."

Fighting spread to the siblings and kept breaking out like a woods fire all day. Pearl found herself going to the window, looking out. She was afraid for her children, afraid for them all.

"Do they go on like this every Saturday?" she asked Lutie.

"Every Saturday?" Lutie said. "Every day!"

"But through the week they're in school!"

"Those two don't go to school half the time. They don't like it. Don't any of my kids." Lutie dried a glass matter-of-factly.

Pearl helped cook, clean, and boil diapers. Danny came in crying with a knot on his forehead. The hard ball hit him, he said. Sister came in and wouldn't go back out. She sat in a big upholstered chair, hands tucked beneath the cushion. Once she came to Pearl. "When are we going home, Mama?" she whispered.

The day dragged on to dusk, then dark. When Buck wasn't back by bedtime, Lutie began to yawn. "Let's turn on in," she said.

Pearl was ready, but she didn't fall asleep at once as she had the night before. The feeling of justification she'd brought up the hill was fading a little. Still, she couldn't get over what Asa had done. She simply couldn't understand how he did it. They didn't need a television, no matter what he said. What they needed was a washing machine so she could wash their clothes, or a tractor to make a living. What if her back gave out so she couldn't wash? Would they sit watching television dirty, like white trash?

Sometime in the night, a pounding on the door awoke her. "Open the goddamn door!" Buck roared from outside.

Lutie's bare feet hurried across the front room floor. The door opened and shut.

Once inside, Buck's wrath filled the house like a noxious odor. "What did you lock me out for, bitch?"

"I'm sorry, honey," Lutie said. "I didn't want anything to get us."

"Get you?" Buck said. "Who in God's name do you think would want you?"

"Nobody," she soothed. "So come on to bed. Everything's all right."

"Aw right?" Buck said loudly. "I'll show you what's aw'right. Lockin' me out of my own goddamn house!"

"Don't, Buck!" Lutie begged. "Please don't. . . !"

There were sounds of a scuffle and heavy breathing, finally a groan. Something fell to the floor and crashed.

Beside Pearl, Danny and Sister sat up in bed. Sister began to whimper. Without thinking, Pearl got up and ran from the room in her flannel nightgown, past Lutie's older children huddled together on the floor in the hall.

"Don't, Buck!" she cried, as he lifted his hand above Lutie, slumped on the floor, arms over her head for protection. "Buck, don't!"

The heavy hand fell. A slack smile spread across Buck's mouth.

"Why, hey there, Pearl," he said. "I forgot we had company. Come on in. Set down." He looked down at his wife. "So fat she can't stand up," he said, with contempt.

He staggered to an overstuffed chair and sank down, arms hanging over the sides like a hunter's dead game.

Pearl helped Lutie to the couch. As she lowered herself to the cushions, Lutie whispered, "We got to pass him out!"

To Buck, she said loudly, "Want a little drink, hon?"

"Little drink?" Buck snorted. "I want a big drink!"

"I've got you some hid," Lutie said.

"I'll get it," Pearl said quickly. "Let me get it."

"You do that, honey," Buck said. "Do that for ole Buck."

The glass jug she brought, its cork stopper reinforced with folded brown paper, was half filled with yellow corn whiskey. Buck drank from the uptilted mouth, yellow liquid spilling onto his good town jacket. When he set down the jug by his chair, he seemed to forget about Lutie and turned to Pearl.

"Ole Buck has a hard time, Pearl," he said. "All these mouths to feed. It's just work, work, ever day. Ever year another mouth to feed. What's the use? You tell me, what's the use?"

Pearl listened, said nothing.

He shook his head. "First thing you know, Buck's a old man, ready to die. Go on, tell me. What's the use?"

She wanted to tell him she didn't really know, that she had questions of her own she couldn't answer. But before she could speak, he forgot her too. His head lolled to one side. He was asleep and snoring.

Lutie hobbled off to get a quilt.

"Pitiful, idn't he?" she said, as she covered him up.

"Yes, but he's apt to hurt you sometime, idn't he?"

"Apt to," Lutie said. With a hand on the hip that had hit the floor, she ushered her children back to their beds.

Silence blessed the house until morning. The children slept late, then the older ones eased out without waking the young ones. Pearl opened her eyes to daylight. Still, she had breakfast ready when Lutie limped in.

"Now it's me acting like company in my own house," Lutie said. "You shouldn't have done all this."

"Well," Pearl said shyly. "I thought we'd go on home this morning."

"You thought what?" Buck said unexpectedly, from the doorway. "Don't let me run you off now, Pearl. You'll have to overlook me. I've got to quit goin' to town on Saturday. It don't agree with me." He put a hand to his head. "Where's them aspirin tablets, Lutie?"

"Oh, it's not you, Buck." A blush spread hotly over Pearl's face. "We need to get on back and see Asa, I guess."

In spite of his head, Buck laughed. "I had up a bet with Lutie," he said. "I told her you wouldn't stay two days."

"She had me fooled, though," Lutie said. "I thought she was through for good!"

Pearl insisted on washing dishes, then couldn't get away fast enough. She hugged Lutie and shook hands solemnly with Buck.

"I'll not try to thank you all," she said, when he handed her the suitcase. "But there'll come a time I can pay you back."

"Bye, bye," the children called.

They were eager to go, but turned again and again to wave to their cousins, quietly watching for once.

The sun was well up, but trees shaded the narrow road. Leaves parted and shut continually on the commerce of birds. A brown rabbit streaked across the road in front of them, so fast his hops ran together like animation. Pearl walked almost unmindful of her children, doing their best to keep up.

Danny's eyes were the sharpest. "I see a wagon," he said, all at once. Then, excitedly, "I think it's Papa!"

"Ah! I believe it is," Pearl said.

They walked faster to meet him, then stopped and waited as he drove up beside them. He pulled up the mules and looked first at Pearl.

"I come to tell you I've hired out to the sawmill," he said. "I can get it for you quick thata way."

"We'd started home," she said, irrelevantly.

He took the suitcase and pulled them in by the hand, first Sister and Danny, then Pearl. Danny and Sister scurried to the back to sit propped against the wagon bed, their legs straight out on the floor in front of them.

Pearl took her place on the spring seat beside Asa. No one spoke as he slapped the mules with the reins and hurried them to a turning place, then maneuvered them into the opposite direction.

When the turn was complete, Pearl leaned toward him on the seat. "I'd rather you wouldn't hire yourself out," she said, above the sounds of the wagon. "You never did that before."

He turned to look at her. "It'll be just part time," he said, "through the winter. Won't take long."

Straight in the face and deep in the eyes, she looked back at him. Creaking and bumping, through wide country silence, they headed home.

✍ The Parlor Tumblers

Mr. Peterson led the way up the rough, wooden steps to the loft of the old barn behind his house. His grandson, Dan, followed. Dan was ten.

If he'd been alone, Mr. Peterson would have talked his way in, and the birds would have let him come without disturbance. Instead, when he opened the wood-framed wire door, pigeons began flying about in all directions. The air filled with bits of pigeon feed, dried droppings, and dusty shed feathers, so that he had to shut his eyes against it. Not the best introduction, he knew.

He was afraid to look down at Dan, the grandson he hadn't seen in three long years. When he and Mrs. Peterson met him at the airport yesterday, Mr. Peterson could tell right away that the old closeness between them was no longer there. Dan hadn't once called him Daddy Pete as before, hadn't called him anything except You.

And when Dan looked at him that first time in the airport, Mr. Peterson recalled the disillusion he'd felt years ago. He'd gone back to see an old teacher, his number-one childhood hero. What he'd found was a pathetic old man, not at all the idol in his memory.

"Well, Dan," he said, when the dust began to settle. "This is it. My dovecote!"

"Your what?"

"My pigeon house." Mr. Peterson chuckled. "In story-books they're sometimes called dovecotes."

The space they stood in, enclosed all around with chicken wire, was partitioned into wire compartments the size of small bedroom closets. In each one, a few nervous pigeons flew back and forth, batting against wire walls, while others peered anxiously from nests built inside wooden boxes.

"I have to separate them like this," Mr. Peterson said, indicating all the compartments, "or they intermate every which way. We try to prevent that."

When Dan said nothing, asked no question in the usual excited voice of children, Mr. Peterson looked down. His grandson was staring curiously, not at the pigeons, but at him.

Mr. Peterson smiled. "I have to tell you something, Dan," he said. "Three things in the world I love. Children, flowers, and birds. Especially grandchildren!"

Dan gave a faint smile as if remembering his manners, but the expression that had settled on his face, soon after they picked him up at the airport, remained.

Dan's father, Mr. and Mrs. Peterson's son Johnny, was a top-notch electrical engineer, just back from large petroleum projects in France and Holland, now on his way to more of the same in California. Johnny had married a wealthy girl from Virginia, and they were living the kind of life he'd always aspired to. They had two daughters younger than Dan.

Mr. Peterson opened the door to one of the compartments and pulled a bird from the air as by sleight of hand. He held it out by pinioned wings.

"Want to hold it?" he asked.

Most children loved to hold the pigeons, cradling them close to their bodies and stroking the feathers for as long as he'd let them.

Dan took the bird but, frowning and squinting, held it out and away from him, so that the frightened bird struggled to get free. As if to erase the whole thing, Mr. Peterson quickly took back the bird, put it in its pen, and moved on.

He opened another door, lowered his head, and stepped into the compartment.

"Did you ever hear the term 'pretty pigeon'?" he asked through the wire. "Here's where it comes from, I think." He looked at the birds around him. "These are the Modenas. Aren't they beautiful?"

The Modenas appeared to be conscious of their beauty. Small and compactly shaped, with iridescent gray feathers, they walked around like prissy little girls, turning their heads this way and that as if for applause.

But when Dan's face remained as closed as ever, Mr. Peterson came right out. Before the next variety, he paused but didn't go in.

"These are for squab," he said, now like a hasty tour guide. "A person could make a little money raising squab, but I never had the heart for it." He shook his head. "I keep them for your grandmother. She likes to have squab now and then, and it's a kind of delicacy she doesn't have much of."

"But . . .?" Dan hesitated.

Mr. Peterson leaned down encouragingly. "Yes, sir?"

"What good are all these pigeons?"

Mr. Peterson laughed. "That's a good question, and you're not the first to ask it. Out loud, at least." He smoothed down his hair with a pale, brown-splotched hand. "It's just a hobby, I guess. Something I enjoy. I always liked fooling with birds. Why, I couldn't tell you."

"But don't you work, or anything?"

Mr. Peterson laughed again. "Your grandmother says I don't, when she's mad at me."

"So my Dad has to send you money every month?"

"He does send a small amount, yes. And we appreciate it very much, but he doesn't have to. How did you know that?"

"My mother told us."

"I see." Mr. Peterson sighed.

"Most of my life I did work, hard," he said. "I taught school out in the country, because I thought that's where they needed me. But I didn't get rich doing it, you understand. I helped your Dad through Georgia Tech, though, and we gave your Aunt Marge a good education. After that, my heart tried to play out. So all I can do now is piddle, it looks like."

He reached under a hen on a nest, brought out an egg, held it up to the light for inspection.

"We could make out just fine on the income we have," he said. "But your Dad doesn't want your grandmother to skimp too much. She's a mighty sweet lady, you know."

He straightened up and brushed himself off. "One more thing and we'll go," he said.

He entered a compartment in the downward slope of the roof and lowered himself into a squatting position. He was surrounded now by large, somewhat clumsy birds of a brownish-red color.

"Watch this!" he said, and clapped his hands.

Almost at once, one of the pigeons turned a somersault backward. It somersaulted again, and again. Mr. Peterson clapped, and several other birds joined the acrobatics, seeming to stimulate each other.

"These are my Tumblers," he said. "They're called Parlor Tumblers, because they don't fly. They can't fly, can't even get off the ground."

Dan had come close to the wire and watched with serious interest. Most of the pigeons were now tumbling backward on the floor.

"Why can't they fly?" he wanted to know.

"It's just the breed, Danboy. The way they were born."

"And you like them?"

"Like them? Yes, very much. In a way, they're the most appealing of all to me, because they're helpless, totally dependent on their keeper. They couldn't fly off in the woods and fend for themselves, for instance, like the others could if they had to."

He caught a Tumbler and held it close. "Besides, I feel closer to them, I guess. I never quite got off the ground myself."

Like a circus performer at the end of his act, he let the bird loose, came out, and latched the wire door behind him.

"Have you got anything else?" Dan asked in a small, plaintive voice. "Besides pigeons?"

"Well, I've got flowers, but not much in bloom. Do you like roses?"

"Yes, sir. I like them all right, but I don't want to see any." Dan sighed. "My other Grandad has a sports car he lets me steer on country roads."

"Is that a fact? Well, we don't have a sports car, but we've got a good old Chevrolet, and I'll take you out and let you steer it all you want to. We'll do whatever you want to do while you're here. Just say the word and we'll do it, if we can!"

"Well, are there any kids around here?" Dan asked hopefully.

"Kids?" Mr. Peterson's eyes widened and lit up. "You bet your boots there are! And they're friends of mine, too. In fact, we've invited some over to meet you, right after this. Your grandmother's in there now making her famous brownies. Can you give me one more minute?"

He hurried into a compartment he'd passed over until now, and pushed up a trap door in the roof. Coming out, he brushed of his hands.

"So let's go," he said.

Outside, he took a whistle from the pocket of his plaid cotton shirt. It was the kind of whistle that coaches use. All those years he'd taught school, he'd had to double as coach as well, baseball, basketball, even football. He blew the whistle loudly, as for a foul of some kind.

Almost at once the back door opened, and Mrs. Peterson came onto the small back porch. She wore a fresh blue dress, with a flower-sprigged apron tied around her waist. Her hair was as soft and white as bubble bath.

"Mother?" Mr. Peterson called out. "How much time do we have?"

"About fifteen minutes," she called back. With a smile and quick little wave, she went back in.

From the old barn, Mr. Peterson brought out a tall stool. Testing with care, he located a level spot on the ground, placed the stool, and steadied it.

"Now," he said. "Would you sit here for a minute, please, sir?"

Dan climbed up and Mr. Peterson squatted on the ground beside him. "Down here in the South we have leaners, hunkerers, and squatters," he said. "I'm a squatter."

Looking down at Mr. Peterson, Dan suddenly grinned. Deep in his eyes, Mr. Peterson could see something beginning at last to thaw.

Meanwhile, a flock of pigeons had erupted through the trap door in the roof. They were now circling around, more or less together, overhead.

The sky was a cloudless blue. The air smelled of newly cut grass. This was the Wayside Community, too far from town to be a suburb, too small to be anything more. Of the families who lived here, some were old like the Petersons, some young with children Dan's age and younger. A combination grocery store and gas station on the highway saved trips to town.

Mr. Peterson pointed up to where the birds were circling higher. "Watch close now!" he said.

Soon a lone pigeon, very high, flipped over and began to fall, as if it had been shot. But it caught itself and flipped over again, and again. Between heart-stopping drops, it flipped several more times before leveling off to fly away.

"Boy!" Dan cried, as other pigeons began doing the same thing. "Look at that!"

"These are the Rollers," Mr. Peterson said, "They're stunt flyers. They do their tricks in the air instead of on the ground like the Tumblers."

Dan had left the stool to stand with his head back, watching.

"Stop!" he yelled out, as one bird rolled and dropped farther and farther down. "Stop that!"

"Sometimes they can't stop," Mr. Peterson said gently.

Dan turned to stare at him. "So what happens?"

"Well, they hit the roof of the house, or the barn. Sometimes the ground."

"Does it hurt?"

"Knocks them out, at times."

"Kills them?"

Mr. Peterson hesitated. "Now and then," he said. "Not often. Usually, they come to and roll again the next time!"

Dan had moved closer to Mr. Peterson. During the more daring stunts above, he held his breath. When one pigeon seemed unable to stop, he covered his eyes and groaned.

"It's all right." Mr. Peterson put a hand on his shoulder, gave a consoling pat. "They love what they're doing. It's what they're bred to do, the way bird dogs are bred to hunt birds."

When one pigeon caught and saved himself at what seemed the last minute, Dan hit Mr. Peterson with his fist and spun around laughing.

Side by side they stood and watched, absorbed as by high-wire performers in a circus, until Mrs. Peterson came back to the door.

"Better come wash up, boys," she called. "My brownies are ready, and your company will be here any minute. Also Amy. I invited Amy."

On their way back to the small, neat house where the Petersons had lived since his retirement, Dan looked up at his grandfather.

"Daddy Pete," he said, "My Dad never told me you had all these pigeons."

"Well, I didn't have them when your Dad was growing up," Mr. Peterson said. "I didn't have time. Besides, your Dad was a smart, ambitious boy who always wanted to do well and amount to something. He wouldn't have liked any messy old birds."

"Not even the Rollers?"

"Well, maybe the Rollers. He was a kind of Roller himself, you know. He wanted to be up there doing his stuff with the best of them. He was never content on the ground, like me."

He ushered Dan into the homey kitchen, which smelled of cleanness, fresh baking, and chocolate.

"I don't know how we ever had your Dad," he told Dan, as he closed the door behind them, "but we're mighty proud we did. Aren't we, Mother?"

Mrs. Peterson was busily arranging sandwiches on a tray, filling tall glasses with ice. "I didn't hear what you said," she answered, "but I'm sure I agree. What I do hear is company at the front door. So hurry up and wash your dirty hands while I go and let them in."

✒ A Good Heart

THEY MET AT THE BACK YARD clothesline of the duplex apartment, two young women in their early twenties. This was before Ames College became a university, and before the town doubled, then tripled, in size.

Sarah, who had just moved in, introduced herself. "I'm Sarah Ingram, from next door."

"Pleased to meet you," her neighbor said pleasantly, in unexpected country dialect. "I'm Miz Wilson."

"We're newcomers," Sarah said. "My husband's a teacher at the college."

"My husband, Robert, he works at the picture show." Mrs. Wilson smiled and a dimple appeared in one smooth cheek. "Works all night and sleeps all day, I tell him."

"You have an adorable baby," Sarah said. She'd seen them together outside.

"That's Little Robert, in there taking his nap. He's my heart." Mrs. Wilson began to pin diapers on the line. She was a natural blonde, without makeup or fixup. Beautiful, Sarah thought.

"How long you been married?" she wanted to know.

"Two years now," Sarah said.

Mrs. Wilson gave her a sideways grin. "Time you had one, idn't it?"

Sarah told Phillip when he came home to lunch, and he laughed. "And what did you say to that?" he asked.

"She's nice, though," Sarah said. "I like her."

The liking grew. After being with other faculty wives, all bright, ambitious, set on helping their husbands to full professorships or tenure, Sarah enjoyed being with someone out of the running. Mrs. Wilson didn't know and didn't care about anything except Robert, Little Robert, and where to save a penny on groceries. She could quote the price of shortening, soap, canned goods and meat from every grocery store in town.

Sarah began to drop in for short visits while Robert was at work. Mrs. Wilson would go on folding diapers or ironing.

"I told Robert the other night," she said one day, "Miz Ingram is not stuck up one bit."

"Well, why should I be?"

Mrs. Wilson was ironing, touching up the collar of a shirt. "You're in Society," she said.

"I wish you'd call me Sarah," Sarah said later. "Everybody else does."

Mrs. Wilson had never told her own first name, not even indirectly. "Oh, I couldn't hardly change now," she said. "I've done got use to it."

The Wilsons came to be in Sarah's consciousness like the time of day and the weather. She turned down the radio when Little Robert was sleeping, set the alarm clock on a pillow so as not to wake Robert. Coming back from a party in the late afternoon, she'd think of Mrs. Wilson at home cooking, ironing, nursing, all that time. When she drove off with Phillip at night, she'd look back at the lonely light next door.

"She never has any fun," she said to Phillip one night. "How do you suppose she stands it?"

"Maybe she gets a kick out of keeping house for old Robert," he joked. "Besides, people like that have their own idea of fun. It may not be the same as ours."

"What do you mean, 'people like that'?" she said defensively. "They're just people like everybody else."

In the light of the dashboard he looked at her fondly. "Well, I wouldn't worry about it too much if I were you. Mrs. Wilson looks pretty happy to me, like she is."

"But she doesn't have any friends."

"She has you and the postman!"

It was true about the postman. If Mrs. Wilson had no friends here, she was in constant touch with the ones at home in Mississippi. She seldom spent a day without a letter, "Return in five days to" penciled into the upper left-hand corner. Sometimes, from a page of lined tablet-paper, she read a piece of news, bad wreck or murder, out loud to Sarah. And she never failed to meet the postman.

"Watch out for rain," she'd tell him. "I heard it on the radio."

"I'm looking for it," he'd say. "My corns are killing me."

Past middle age, heavy on his feet, he'd smile beneath a meaty forehead and hand her a letter. If she wasn't holding Little Robert, he'd want to know how that big boy was doing today. To Sarah, he was all Postal Service, on the job and busy.

Staying in touch was mainly up to Sarah, since Mrs. Wilson was clearly not at ease in the Ingram apartment.

"Why do you always leave when Phillip comes home?" Sarah complained. "He'll never get to know you!"

"Lord, I wouldn't crack my lips around that man," Mrs. Wilson said.

"Why on earth not?"

"And him a English teacher? I don't know how to talk, and I know it."

"But Phillip doesn't care!"

"Well, he might not, but I do."

As with the use of names, nothing changed.

Sarah kept wanting to do something for Mrs. Wilson, some little something to relieve the monotony of her days. She thought the Wilsons must be strict sectarians of one kind or another, so she offered to keep Little Robert so they could go to church some Sunday.

"Lord, Robert wouldn't darken the door of no church," Mrs.

Wilson said at once. "He hasn't been to church since his Daddy whipped him and made him go when he was little. We had to get married in the courthouse."

By now Sarah had been to Coca-Cola parties, cocktail parties, teas, dinners, and picnics, so it was payback time. The weather cooled off, and she had a new recipe for spiced tea. She decided to invite fifteen or so women for a simple afternoon get-together.

When she thought of Mrs. Wilson, next door but left out, she decided to ask her to come and help serve. She wouldn't have to talk, just smile, Sarah told her. She could bring Little Robert in his stroller. Everyone would enjoy him, and when he got tired he could take his nap on her bed.

"Mark it on your calendar now, so you won't forget," she said.

Sarah spent a week getting ready. She washed windows, waxed the floor of her living-dining room on her hands and knees. She polished silver and got out wedding china. The day before the party, she made cookies.

Mrs. Wilson, who'd been curiously checking all preparations, dropped in as she was taking a sheet of cookies from the oven.

Sarah didn't make cookies often. She was still in the learning stage of baking. For her, possible disaster lay in every step. Her face was hot from the oven and from effort. Her sink was stacked with bowls and utensils to be washed.

Standing, looking on with folded arms, Mrs. Wilson shook her head. "Lord, I wouldn't go to all that trouble for nobody."

Anyone else would lend a hand, Sarah thought, as Mrs. Wilson turned to go. So far she hadn't helped or even offered to help, at all.

"Well, come early tomorrow," she said. She'd already showed her what to do, mainly in the kitchen.

Next morning, she made party-size sandwiches. Phillip's lunch was refrigerator scraps and a Coke, but she let him have one of each kind of sandwich and a cookie.

She was ready, dressed, and wearing fresh lipstick when her first guests arrived. She was also nervous, a newcomer about to be judged. The judgement would be superficial, she knew, and would neither make nor break Phillip. Still, it would affect him in its way.

Her guests quickly put her at ease. They loved what she'd done with the apartment, they said, and were delighted to have a couple so young and bright at Ames. So everything was going to be all right, she felt.

Only, where was Mrs. Wilson? She'd counted on her to bring in sandwiches and cookies. She was hastily uncovering trays in the kitchen when the face of a guest appeared around the door.

"Need some help?"

"Golly, yes!"

"Here, let me do that."

Cups were filled and refilled, plates served and replenished. Voices rose and fell like an orchestra in practice. From time to time, there was a burst of laughter.

Someone finally looked at a watch and gasped. Like birds from a feeder, they left in a flurry.

Sarah went straight to the phone to call Mrs. Wilson. "What happened?" she wanted to know.

Mrs. Wilson sounded miles away, like a stranger or even wrong number. "I couldn't make it this time," she said.

Sarah waited for explanation, white lie, something, but the line continued to buzz with silence.

"Well, I missed you," she said, and hung up.

She didn't tell Phillip, even when he noticed her mood.

"Did something go wrong?" he asked, eating sandwich after sandwich and a big tomato, on his way to cookies and toasted pecans.

"No, everything was fine, and I think they all enjoyed it. I'm just worn out," she said, and began gathering up tea napkins to be washed.

She tried to put herself in Mrs. Wilson's place, to think what might have happened, but it was beyond her. She didn't understand it, and she didn't like it.

So she'd stop seeing Mrs. Wilson, she decided. After all, they had nothing in common. They were women and human beings who happened to be neighbors, which could have been everything but was not enough, it seemed.

She began with avoidance. Clothes she'd have hung on the line, she hung on a rack in the apartment. She went in and out when she knew Mrs. Wilson was busy inside. And Mrs. Wilson made no overtures, as if she understood.

"What's become of your little friend next door?" Phillip wanted to know. "I haven't seen her lately."

"I haven't either," said Sarah.

But one morning she was walking home with a bag of groceries and Mrs. Wilson was sitting on the front stoop waiting for the postman. There was no way around her.

"You been to Gleason's?" Mrs. Wilson asked, as pleasantly as ever.

"No, the Super Market."

"Did you get some of them cheap T-bones?"

"No. No, I didn't."

Sarah smiled, but went straight inside and closed the door. Almost at once, she was sorry. After all, she had no friends here either. Not the close, comfortable kind it took a while to make. Those, she'd left behind. Now, when she wasn't busy she was lonely —except for Phillip, who spent most of his time in a classroom or his office, more accessible to students than to her, she sometimes felt.

The next morning was cold, coldest of the year so far. She went to hang an afghan, just out of mothballs, on the line to air. It was a brilliant day, the kind that tends to minimize everything except itself. She wasn't even thinking of Mrs. Wilson when a back door slammed and there she was, hands full of dishtowels wrung into hard, wet spirals.

"I seen that pretty thing on the line through the window," she said. "My Aunt Myrtle's got one she crocheted herself."

"Has she?" Sarah turned to go back inside.

But Mrs. Wilson stopped her. "How was your party?"

"Fine," Sarah said. "It was fine."

"I know you was mad because I didn't come." Still holding wet towels, Mrs. Wilson paused. "But to tell you the truth, I didn't have nothing to wear. I didn't have nothing and Robert said that, with that baby, we couldn't afford no new clothes. So I just didn't come."

Sarah felt a pulse beating strongly in her throat. "You could have worn anything," she said. "As pretty as you are, it wouldn't have mattered."

Mrs. Wilson shook her head. "No, I'd of embarrassed me and you both."

Back in the kitchen Sarah poured herself a cup of leftover coffee. How could she have been so blind? It was true that she'd never seen Mrs. Wilson dressed up. But she would have thought, if she'd thought, that she had something to wear to a funeral, at least. Sitting at the kitchen table she stared into space, trying to absorb what she'd learned. The coffee in her cup had been too long in the pot, but she drank it, black and bitter.

Winter settled in at last, and everyone moved inside. On East Magnolia Street, gas space heaters glowed day and night. In the Wilson apartment, Little Robert cried with head colds and fretted from being kept indoors all day. Mrs. Wilson's face, when Sarah saw her bringing in armloads of diapers, was stoically set.

"Did you know it got down to eighteen last night?" she was telling the postman one morning, as Sarah popped out to get her mail.

"Oh, yes. Yes, ma'am! That wind is like a knife." His eyes were watering. Drops sat on his cheeks like tears as he handed Mrs. Wilson a letter.

In Sarah's box he'd left only bills. She put them on Phillip's desk and decided to go next door for a minute. Seeing Little Robert always cheered her up. He made her look to the future.

Little Robert was asleep, but Mrs. Wilson was wide-awake, still holding the letter she'd just brought in. In her living room no lights were on, but her eyes were glowing.

"I'm goin' home this week end!" she announced excitedly. "Mama and Papa, they've been married fifty years Sunday, and it'll be a big to-do."

"Oh, a Golden Wedding!" Sarah caught the excitement.

"My oldest sister, the one that runs the beauty shop, she just sent my bus fare." Mrs. Wilson indicated the letter in her hand. "Robert couldn't get off from the show, so I'd done wrote I couldn't come."

"Let me keep Little Robert for you!" Sarah offered.

Mrs. Wilson laughed. "Lord, they wouldn't let me in at the door without him!"

"Well, what can I do to help you?"

Mrs. Wilson shook her head. Sarah knew that in her mind she was already on a bus, bound for Mississippi.

What she needed most, Sarah thought, was something to wear. Since the party, she'd noticed her clothes. Besides everyday slacks and sweaters, all but worn out, she had a badly sprung skirt and a blouse ironed so often it looked brittle. She had an old jacket of Robert's that she wore outside at home, and a thin navy coat she wore to town. That was it.

Back in her apartment, she opened the door to her closet. She had a good Sunday coat, a red coat she wore most of the time, and the coat she'd worn in college, still in fair shape.

She pushed back hangers to a pale yellow silk dress she'd had before she married. Just the thing for a Golden Wedding, she thought, the minute she saw it. The shoulder pads and hemline were slightly dated now, but the style itself was timeless. It would be just right on Mrs. Wilson, who was taller and thinner than she was.

"Phillip," she said that night. "Do you think it would hurt Mrs. Wilson's feelings if I offered to lend her something to wear?"

He stopped grading papers to look at her and listen. "No, honey. I don't think you'd hurt Mrs. Wilson's feelings. It's your own feelings you'd better think about, in my opinion."

Robert had to be at work when it was time to go, so Mrs. Wilson called a taxi to take her to the bus. Sarah went over to help her get off. She carried the diaper bag and suitcase, while Mrs. Wilson carried Little Robert, bundled up so that only his face showed. With her shoulder-length hair just washed, her face all smiles and dancing dimple, Mrs. Wilson was wearing Sarah's red coat.

"She looked like a million dollars when she got in that taxi," Sarah told Phillip that night. "Really."

"Until she opened that mouth," he said.

She didn't tell him she'd loaned Mrs. Wilson the yellow dress too. Phillip loved that dress. She hadn't worn it in a while, but she hadn't retired it either. The first night she wore it, he'd given a modified wolf whistle when she came out.

The weekend went by quickly. Each time Sarah put on her old college coat, she thought of Mrs. Wilson back home in Mississippi, having the time of her life at the Golden Wedding. She couldn't wait to hear all about it.

But she didn't see Mrs. Wilson the day she got home. She knew she was there and expected to hear from her any minute. She was disappointed when she didn't but, remembering the party, she knew there was a reason.

She was sure Mrs. Wilson would come the next morning. Once she even stopped and listened to hurrying footsteps next door, thinking now she's on the way. But by lunchtime she'd heard nothing. Soon after, when she saw Mrs. Wilson hanging out clothes, she put on a jacket and hurried out.

"Hey, there," she called above a wind that, when it gusted, held things horizontal on the line.

Mrs. Wilson might have been watching the approach of a stranger.

"Is everything all right?" Sarah asked, coming closer.

Mrs. Wilson gave a dubious nod.

"Is Little Robert okay?"

"Fine."

"Well, how was the Golden Wedding?" Sarah asked impatiently.

"It was nice." Mrs. Wilson spoke as if invisibly nudged into speech. "Aunt Myrtle had a big cake baked. Not in layers but in . . . I can't think of the word."

"Tiers?"

Mrs. Wilson nodded and went on. "The photographer come and made pictures. They're going to have one put in the paper."

She turned back to the clothesline and began to retreat, a diaper at a time. Sarah waited until she'd hung the last one and started back inside.

"It'll take me a week to clean up that pig sty," she said, hurrying by Sarah. "That Robert dirtied up everything on the place while we was gone."

By now Sarah knew that something was wrong. Was it something about the clothes?

She waited another day, then resolved to go and ask. In her mind she set a time like an appointment. When it came, she went to Mrs. Wilson's kitchen door and knocked.

Mrs. Wilson seemed to search for a smile and be unable to find one. "Let's go up in the living room," she said.

"I can't stay." Sarah said. "I just wondered if you were through with those clothes."

"I was intending to bring them clothes home today," Mrs. Wilson said in a rush. "I sent that coat to the cleaners so it wouldn't smell baby, and there was a little spot on the dress." She seemed to run out of breath. "I'll get 'em."

While she waited, feeling like a landlord or bill collector, Sarah looked at the old gas stove, dented coffeepot, and limp plastic curtains. Dishes were washed and counter tops wiped off, but there was a lingering smell of frying and used grease.

"Thanks," she said, when Mrs. Wilson brought the clothes in a brown cleaning bag.

"Mama asked me where I got them pretty clothes," Mrs. Wilson said. "I told her I had a neighbor with a real good heart!"

Back in her bedroom, Sarah hung the clothes on her open closet door and carefully took off the brown bag. The red coat smelled of cleaning fluid, but looked as if it might have been washed in water.

One button was missing. She felt quickly in the pockets but it wasn't there. Besides the spot Mrs. Wilson mentioned, the yellow dress had deep underarm stains from perspiration.

Helplessly, she looked at her clothes. She could see Little Robert spitting-up on the coat and Mrs. Wilson, perspiring with excitement, spilling punch on the dress. Clearest of all, she could see Mrs. Wilson, back from Mississippi, going to the cheapest cleaner in town.

There was only one thing she could do about it at the moment, and she did it. She sat down on her bed and cried.

$\mathscr{L}$ A Meeting on the Road

ONE JANUARY MORNING in 1995, in the small town of Ashton, Alabama, Ben Neighbors, a white lawyer, checked his watch. Nine-forty.

The newly elected County Commission, with a black majority for the first time since Reconstruction, would meet in twenty minutes. Ben had held the job of legal counsel to the Commission for the past ten years and wanted to be early for the meeting. On the way, he was stopped by a client and had to wait and listen, give advice.

When he reached the courthouse, a columned antebellum building that dominated the town, the meeting was about to begin. Five men, three black and two white, were already seated around an oblong table down front, in the old-fashioned main courtroom upstairs.

On the far side of the table, the two whites sat together, the black chairman at the head, and a reelected black on his left. The black member at the foot, newly elected, had been the playmate and best friend, Ben had thought, of his lonely childhood. Later on, he'd left Ashton to come back changed. Ben didn't know what he was like now.

He eased into a row of folding seats near the table and placed his files on an empty seat beside him. The new Commission would make changes, he knew, some major, but his job would be the same. To him, the law was the law and he never tried to bend it.

Immediately after the call to order and opening prayer, he was surprised when the black chairman turned to him with a smile.

"We have a change for you, Mr. Attorney," the chairman said. He pushed back the printed agenda in front of him. "From now on, we want all your opinions in writing. If we have them on paper we'll be protected, you understand." He leaned back in his chair and smiled again. "I think that's all for you today, so we'll excuse you."

Ben's head roared as if landing on a plane. Written opinions? Like all county attorneys that he knew, or knew of, he'd given oral opinions while the Board was in session, and on the phone when it wasn't, the only way to do it as far as he knew.

He stood up to protest, but didn't trust himself to speak. Instead, he picked up his files and walked quickly from the court-room, hardly noticing anyone he passed.

What was this all about?, he wondered, hurrying down the stairs and out of the old building. And what did they mean, protected? Were they saying that they didn't trust him, that they thought he might go back on his word, or cause trouble in some way? He'd been totally honest and fair, and they knew it.

Outside, the day was unseasonably warm, like spring, but few people were out on the street. Barton's, the only clothing store still left in town, had a Sale sign out front as usual. Down the street by the liquor store, a group of black loiterers leaned against a boarded-up store front. Two white women in old, sagging sweaters were going through a rack of clothing priced for clearance outside the Dollar Store. Ben waited at the curb until the traffic light changed, then hurried across the street to his office.

The minute the meeting was over, he had a phone call from Fred Walker, one of the whites still not unseated.

"They fired you, Ben, quick as you left the room," Fred said. He was out of breath, his voice high-pitched. "There was a motion to replace you, right off the bat. Three aye's, two nay's, and you were out." He paused. "They gave the job to Tyree, same way. But they want you to resign, in a letter. For the minutes."

Something in Ben's chest tightened and held. Tyree was a black lawyer, young, who'd just come to town. He'd practiced for less than a year.

"What about written opinions?" he asked.

"Oh, that was just to get you out so they could fire you, I guess. It wasn't mentioned again."

Two days went by and Ben felt worse, not better. When the subject came up, he smiled, shrugged, and kept his mouth shut, but he couldn't sleep at night. It was on his mind all day. He felt suddenly old and tired at fifty.

He'd miss the job, he knew, regular income, good benefits. With a son in college and daughter in private school, he'd be forced to take whatever cases came in his door from now on. Some, with obvious legal pitfalls, he'd stayed out of in the past. Already, he lived in fear of being sued for malpractice, of losing everything he owned because of some honest mistake that got by him.

There was nothing he could do except take what they'd done, he knew, so he meant to take it with as much grace as possible, and get on with his life. But he couldn't control the feelings inside him, like an angry crowd yelling and protesting, trying to get out.

On the third afternoon, hoping that exercise would help, he went home to walk before dark. He lived six miles from Ashton and walked, when he could, on orders from his doctor. A non-smoker, never overweight, even-tempered by nature, he'd developed high blood pressure against the odds. Sometimes it was much too high, and today was one of the times, he suspected.

The day was still warm, almost hot, so he went by home first to change to a short-sleeved shirt. His house, a spacious one-story design with cupola and wrap-around porch, had been built with slave labor before the Civil War. Built by the grandfather for whom he was named, it had been lived in by members of his family, through good times and bad, ever since. Wind still rattled the windows and froze them in winter. Something always needed fixing, replacing, or painting. But Ben loved it, house, deep shady lawn, old trees and camellia bushes, scuppernong arbor. The house and land around it were the reasons he'd come back to Ashton, to hang out his shingle and stay on. It was his home.

Down the lane on the paved county road, he rotated his arms to loosen his shoulders and took a deep breath to relax. With him was Dan, his favorite bird dog, also his best watch dog, a large liver-spotted pointer trotting along up ahead.

With no traffic on the road, he was soon walking automatically, his mind on the firing as before. In the clear, non-partisan air, he hoped to replace emotion with reason and stop the turmoil inside him. Ashton was a black town now, he told himself bluntly, and whites could expect from them what they'd received in the past. He could stay and accept it, or leave. And leaving would be hard at his age. He couldn't pick up and move his practice, like a load of furniture. Not to mention house and land.

His grandfathers had farmed the land and survived, even prospered. But his father, an only child, had gone into law, then politics, high life and drinking, and wound up the prodigal. He would have lost the whole place, had not Ben's mother, a slight, earnest figure raised on a Texas ranch, stepped in to take over.

To everyone's amazement, she'd turned the farm into a cattle farm and saved it. Longtime cattlemen and cowboys tipped their hats to her and called her "Miss Judy." At the weekly stockyard auction following her death, they had all stood for a moment of silence to honor, the auctioneer said, "a great lady and great cattlewoman."

But cattle had declined, along with everything else around Ashton, and the stockyard had closed. With no option at the time, he'd leased the land to a packing company for pasture at a giveaway price.

He walker harder, faster, eyes on the road, trying to reconcile the present with the past, and to somehow foresee the future.

All those years that his mother ran the farm, Easter Agee, a black woman, had looked after him. Cooks and maids came and went in the household, but Easter was there all the time. When he awoke as a child, his mother was already out on the place, or off somewhere on farm business. Easter gave him breakfast, dinner, supper, and saw him through the day. In summer she took him to hunt plums and berries, to fish in a creek. In winter they made pull-candy and a few memorable bowls of snow ice cream.

When he was sick, she sat by his bed and sang, about Little David and his harp, cracklin' bread, sweet chariots. Sometimes she simply hummed, from deep in her soul, until he fell asleep to wake up feeling better.

"Your son talks like a pickaninny!" his father had said to his mother one night, out on the porch. He was home from he legislature, a drink in his hand as usual. "How do you stand it?"

He'd thought Ben was asleep in the swing.

"Who do you expect him to talk like?" his mother had said sharply. "You? He never sees you." In a sad, tired voice, she'd added, "Nor me either, for that matter."

In the swing, Ben had started to cry. When his father picked him up, he couldn't stop crying.

"I want Easter," he'd sobbed.

When he was five, to lighten Easter's load but by no means free her, Henry Philpot, a black boy on the place, who was ten, had been his daily playmate. Each morning after breakfast, he'd sat on the back steps to wait for Henry.

They'd built a ramshackle lean-to out of old scrap lumber. The club house, they called it, and played in it, carried food out to eat in it, spent rainy days dodging the leaks in it. When they outgrew it, no one had the heart to tear it down, and it had stood in the back yard like a scarecrow until the wind blew it over.

If he was given a baseball glove, Henry got a mitt. Henry's bicycle was less expensive, but seemed to go faster.

"You the best, though," Henry would say, still out of breath, each time he won a race or game. "You the best!"

"I'm not the best!" he'd burst out one day. "What makes you say that? You beat me every time."

Henry had leaned down and picked up a rock. "Muh-dear told me to let you win," he said. "You white."

Now Henry was the new commissioner, the one who made the motion to replace him, Fred said.

"Henry did?" he'd asked, to be sure.

"Right. Henry Philpot. Grew up out there on your place."

Ben remembered a hot summer Saturday in the sixties when he'd watched the start of a new demonstration. A worn-out white deputy had looked at the black leader he stood facing.

"I wish you'd tell me what it is you all want," the deputy had said like a plea, the back of his shirt wet with sweat already. "What would it take to satisfy you, so we could cut all this out and get back to work?"

The answer, delivered as from a pulpit, had spread like a news flash.

"We want this town, and we want this county. We got the vote, and the law behind us. It's our time now!"

The stretch of road ahead of Ben had just been patched out of season because of a pot-hole accident, for which the county might be sued. The smell of tar was still strong, crushed rocks on top still loose. On his way to work today, a passing car had thrown a rock against his windshield but luckily hadn't cracked it. No one was left in town who could fix it.

Rocks began to crunch beneath his shoes and slow him down. Dan avoided the rocky road by taking to the roadsides and ditches.

Up ahead, something was beginning to emerge from a storm-cloud of rock dust. A red sports car with the top down was coming too fast for the road. Ben soon made out a black driver in wrap-around shades and a dazzling white shirt. Drug dealer, he'd come to think, right or wrong, at the sight of a black in a flashy car.

To give the red car room, he got off the road all the way, onto a shoulder high in dead grass, weeds, and kudzu. He looked to see that Dan was out of the way, but Dan had run off somewhere out of sight.

And the red car was not slowing down, nor leaving the middle of the road. The driver, shades like a glossy mask, looked straight ahead.

A gust of thick gray dust hit Ben all at once. Grit peppered his bare arms and clothes. He shut his eyes and turned his head, but not before a small rock had stung him on the temple, close to one eye.

Instantly, as if transported, he found himself in the middle of the road, shouting after the driver.

"Run over me then, God damn it!"

He was like a radiator boiling over. His chest heaved. If he had a stroke, he didn't care.

"You son of a bitch!" he yelled, then drew himself together, filled his lungs, and hurled his voice like a weapon.

"Go to hell. All of you."

The driver evidently heard yelling, saw someone waving his arms in the middle of the road, and backed to near where Ben stood. Looking puzzled, he got out of his car.

"You hollerin' at me?"

"Damn right!" Ben said hotly. "Who do you think you are, tearing down the road, throwing rocks in people's faces?"

Up close, he could see that the car was secondhand, the white shirt new but not expensive. And the driver was young, maybe thirty. Without the shades, he looked oddly familiar.

"I'm in a hurry, man," the driver said, his accent from somewhere up north.

Ben put a hand to his temple, found a hot little lump. He spat the taste of dust from his mouth.

The stranger frowned, watching. "I'm not used to no Southern roads," he said.

"Well, you're not blind!" Ben shot back. "You saw me and knew to slow down. You just want to run over somebody, all of you, every chance you get!"

The stranger looked at him, said nothing.

"Only a nigger would do something like that!" Ben said. It came out of nowhere, a word he despised, never used, even in jest. He'd winced to hear it all of his life.

A muscle twitched in the young man's cheek. Small flames leapt up in the depths of his eyes. For a split-second he said nothing. Then his voice came hard and tight as a fist.

"You got to 'pologize for that, motherfucker! You better 'pologize now!"

"'Pologize for your goddamn rocks!" Ben said, and stepped forward.

They came at each other, mouths set. Ben was bigger, but the black man was young and quick. Ben's right arm was caught at once in a grip so strong it was all he could do not to cry out, but he twisted and strained, this way and that, until his muscles quivered and the grip began to loosen. He did not intend to be licked. Not if it killed him, today, on this road.

But then Dan was there, with a sound he never heard from him before, the warning growl of a guard dog. From close beside him Dan growled again, deep in his throat, and the man let go and drew back, eyes wide.

Eye to eye, Ben froze, as if a restraining hand had clapped him on the shoulder.

Who was this stranger? He knew those eyes, didn't he? Somber, set wide apart, so still they could be unsettling. And not just the eyes. The features, matte black skin, solid stance. All familiar. He felt his heart stop, clench.

"Are you an Agee?" he asked, and held his breath.

"Say what?"

"Is you name Agee?" Ben cried. "Did you know Easter Agee?"

The stranger hesitated, glanced at the dog. "Easter Agee was my grandma," he said. "But she passed, long ago."

Ben stepped back, arms now limp at his sides. Tears blurred his eyes. A held-back sob distorted his face.

"Easter Agee raised me," he said.

Overhead the drone of a plane grew loud, then faded. In the pasture a calf bleated for its mother, sounding lost. The grandson gave Ben a long, speculative look, then checked the dog now sitting, panting, beside him.

"Say she did?"

It was a comment, Ben knew, not a question. It was closure. The grandson wanted to be on his way. Besides, the last thing he wanted to hear, no doubt, was that his grandmother had been someone's mammy.

Ben fought back the impulse to tell him anyway, as in some crucial summation to a jury, what Easter had meant to him. But things like that weren't said any more. They were considered racist, patronizing, some kind of put-down.

Also, after Henry, he couldn't help wondering how Easter had really felt about him all those years, at night on her lumpy mattress. If her faithfulness hadn't been three parts necessity at the time. Things had been worse for her then than they were for him now.

He looked at her grandson across a no man's land of silence. Behind them on the flat Black Belt prairie, the sun reddened and glared before starting to set. There was no sound except the lonely, drawn-out lowing of a cow soon to be slaughtered.

Ben glanced at the sun, drew a quavering breath, and sighed. "Don't let me hold you up," he said. "You're late already."

The grandson shrugged.

"Well, all right, then," he said, like a schoolboy let out for recess. "I better head on. But I been hearin' about Ashton all my life. I just cut through here to see what it look like."

He hurried back to his car, got in, and shut the door. Before driving off, he looked back at Ben.

"Man, you take it easy," he said. "Okay?"

Ben raised his hand in the semblance of a wave. "Take care," he called out too late, whether to the grandson or himself he didn't know.

The University of Alabama Press

VICKI COVINGTON
Gathering Home

VICKI COVINGTON
The Last Hotel for Women

NANCI KINCAID
Crossing Blood

PAUL HEMPHILL
Leaving Birmingham: Notes of a Native Son

ROY HOFFMAN
Almost Family

HELEN NORRIS
One Day in the Life of a Born Again Loser and Other Stories

PATRICIA FOSTER
All the Lost Girls: Confessions of a Southern Daughter

SAM HODGES
B-4

HOWELL RAINES
Whiskey Man

JUDITH HILLMAN PATERSON
Sweet Mystery: A Book of Remembering

JAY LAMAR AND JEANIE THOMPSON, EDS.
The Remembered Gate: Memoirs by Alabama Writers

MARY WARD BROWN
Tongues of Flame

MARY WARD BROWN
It Wasn't All Dancing and Other Stories

EUGENE WALTER
The Untidy Pilgrim

JULIA OLIVER
Goodbye to the Buttermilk Sky